"I hope I never meet him again."

Julia snipped savagely at a length of curtain intended for a dress.

"Well, I don't suppose you will—he's a bit grand for us...."

"Why do you say he's so grand?"

"He's at the very top of the tree in the medical world and he's got a Dutch title, comes from a very ancient family with lots of money...."

"Huh," said Julia. "Probably no one's good enough for him."

Ruth said mildly, "You *do* dislike him, don't you?"

Betty Neels spent her childhood and youth in
Devonshire before training as a nurse and midwife.
She was an army nursing sister during the war, married a
Dutchman and subsequently lived in Holland for fourteen
years. She lives with her husband in Dorset, England, and
has a daughter and grandson. Her interests are reading,
animals, old buildings and writing. Betty started to write
on retirement from nursing, incited by a lady in a library,
who was bemoaning the lack of romantic novels.

Look out for two wonderful brand-new stories in
The Engagement Effect
by bestselling author Betty Neels
and
RITA-winning author Liz Fielding
Coming next month in Harlequin Romance®
On sale February 2002 (#3689)

BETTY NEELS
An Independent Woman

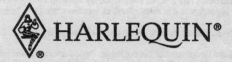

TORONTO • NEW YORK • LONDON
AMSTERDAM • PARIS • SYDNEY • HAMBURG
STOCKHOLM • ATHENS • TOKYO • MILAN • MADRID
PRAGUE • WARSAW • BUDAPEST • AUCKLAND

ISBN 0-373-03685-X

AN INDEPENDENT WOMAN

First North American Publication 2002.

Copyright © 2001 by Betty Neels.

This edition published by arrangement with Harlequin Books S.A.

® and ™ are trademarks of the publisher. Trademarks indicated with ® are registered in the United States Patent and Trademark Office, the Canadian Trade Marks Office and in other countries.

Visit us at www.eHarlequin.com

Printed in U.S.A.

CHAPTER ONE

THE street, like hundreds of other streets in that part of London, was shabby but genteelly so, for the occupants of the small turn-of-the-century houses which lined it had done their best; there were clean net curtains at the windows and the paintwork was pristine, even if badly in need of a fresh coat. Even so, the street was dull under a leaden sky and slippery with the cold sleet.

The girl, Ruth, looking out of the window of one of the houses, frowned at the dreary view and said over her shoulder, 'I don't think I can bear to go on living here much longer...'

'Well, you won't have to—Thomas will get the Senior Registrar's post and you'll marry and be happy ever after.'

The speaker who answered, Julia, was kneeling on the shabby carpet, pinning a paper pattern to a length of material. She was a pretty girl, with a quantity of russet hair tied back carelessly with a bootlace, a tip-tilted nose and a wide mouth. Her eyes under thick brows were grey, and as she got to her feet it was apparent that she was a big girl with a splendid figure.

She wandered over to the window to join her sister. 'A good thing that Dr Goodman hasn't got a surgery this morning; you've no need to go out.'

'The evening surgery will be packed to the doors...'

They both turned their heads as a door opened and another girl, Monica, came in. A very beautiful girl, almost as beautiful as her elder sister. For while Julia, she of the russet hair, was pretty, the other two were both lovely, with fair hair and blue eyes. Ruth was taller than Monica, and equally slender, but they shared identical good looks.

'I'm off. Though heaven knows how many children will turn up in this weather.' Monica smiled. 'But George was going to look in...'

George was the parish curate, young and enthusiastic, nice-looking in a rather crumpled way and very much in love with Monica.

They chorused goodbyes as she went away again.

'I'm going to wash my hair,' said Ruth, and Julia got down onto her knees again and picked up the scissors.

The front doorbell rang as she did so, and Ruth said from the door, 'That will be the milkman; I forgot to pay him...I'll go.'

Professor Gerard van der Maes stood on the doorstep and looked around him. He had, in an unguarded moment, offered to deliver a package from his registrar Thomas, to that young man's fiancée—something which, it seemed, it was vital she received as quickly as possible. Since the registrar was on duty, and unlikely to be free for some time, and the Professor was driving himself to a Birmingham hospital and would need to thread his way through the northern parts of London, a slight deviation from his route was of little consequence.

Now, glancing around him, he rather regretted his offer. It had taken him longer than he had expected to find the house and he found the dreary street not at all to his taste. From time to time he had listened to Thomas's diffident but glowing remarks about his fiancée, but no one had told him that she lived in such a run-down part of the city.

The girl who answered the door more than made up for the surroundings. If this was Ruth, then Thomas must indeed be a happy man.

He held out a hand. 'Van der Maes, a colleague of Thomas. He wanted you to have a parcel and I happened to be going this way.'

'Professor van der Maes.' Ruth beamed up at him. 'How kind of you.' She added, not quite truthfully, 'I was just going to make coffee…'

He followed her into the narrow hall and into the living room and Ruth said, 'Julia…'

'If it's money you want there's some in my purse…' Julia didn't look up. 'Don't stop me or I'll cut too much off.'

'It's Professor van der Maes.'

'Not the old man from across the street?' Julia snipped carefully. 'I knew he'd break a leg one day, going outside in his slippers.'

Ruth gave the Professor an apologetic glance. 'We have a visitor, Julia.'

Julia turned round then, and looked at the pair of them standing in the doorway. Ruth, as lovely as ever, looked put out and her companion looked amused. Julia got to her feet, looking at him. Not quite her idea of a professor: immensely tall and large in his person, dark hair going grey, heavy brows above cold eyes and a nose high-bridged and patrician above a thin mouth. Better a friend than an enemy, thought Julia. Not that he looked very friendly...

She held out a hand and had it gently crushed.

'I'll make the coffee,' said Ruth, and shut the door behind her.

'Do sit down,' said Julia, being sociable.

Instead he crossed the room to stand beside her and look down at the stuff spread out on the carpet.

'It looks like a curtain,' he observed.

'It is a curtain,' said Julia snappishly. It was on the tip of her tongue to tell him that by the time she had finished with it it would be a dress suitable to wear to an annual dance which the firm she worked for gave to its employees. A not very exciting occasion, but it was to be held at one of London's well-known hotels and that, combined with the fact that it was mid-February and life was a bit dull, meant that the occasion merited an effort on her part to make the best of herself.

She remembered her manners. 'Do you know Thomas? I suppose you're from the hospital. He's Ruth's fiancé. He's not ill or anything?'

'I know Thomas and I am at the same hospital. He is in splendid health.'

'Oh, good. But horribly overworked, I suppose?'

'Yes, indeed.' His eye fell on the curtain once more. 'You are a skilled needlewoman?'

'Only when I am desperate. What do you do at the hospital? Teach, I suppose, if you are a professor?'

'I do my best...'

'Of what? Professor of what?'

'Surgery.'

'So you're handy with a needle too!' said Julia, and

before he could answer that Ruth came in with the coffee.

'Getting to know each other?' she asked cheerfully. 'Thank you for bringing the parcel, Professor. I'm sorry you won't see Monica—she runs the nursery school here. Luckily I've got the morning off from the surgery, and Julia is always here, of course. She works at home—writes verses for greetings cards.'

Ruth handed round the coffee, oblivious of Julia's heavy frown.

'How very interesting,' observed the Professor, and she gave him a quick look, suspecting that he was amused. Which he was, although nothing of it showed on his face.

Ruth asked diffidently. 'I suppose Thomas hasn't heard if he's got that senior registrar's job? I know he'd phone me, but if he's busy...'

'I think I can set your mind at rest. He should hear some time today. He's a good man and I shall be glad to have him in my team in a senior capacity.' He smiled at Ruth. 'Does that mean that you will marry?'

She beamed at him. 'Yes, just as soon as we can find somewhere to live.' She went on chattily, 'An aunt left us this house, and we came here to live when Mother and Father died, but I think we shall all be glad when we marry and can leave it.'

'Your other sister—Monica?' encouraged the Professor gently.

'Oh, she's engaged to the local curate; he's just waiting to get a parish. And Julia's got an admirer—a junior partner in the firm she works for. So you see, we are all nicely settled.'

He glanced at Julia. She didn't look at all settled,

for she was indignantly pink and looked as though she wanted to throw something. She said coldly, 'I'm sure the Professor isn't in the least interested in us, Ruth.' She picked up the coffee pot. 'More coffee, Professor?'

Her tone dared him to say yes and delay his departure.

He had a second cup, and she hated him. And she thought he would never go.

When he did, he shook hands, with the observation that the dress would be a success.

Ruth went with him to the door. When she came back she said, 'He's got a Rolls; you ought to see it.' She glanced at Julia's kneeling form. 'You were a bit rude, dear. And he's such a nice man.'

Julia snipped savagely at a length of curtain. 'I hope I never meet him again.'

'Well, I don't suppose you will. He's a bit grand for us...'

'There's nothing wrong with a rising young surgeon and a member of the clergy.' She'd almost added *and a junior partner in a greetings card firm,* but she didn't, for Oscar, accepted as her admirer by everyone but herself, didn't quite fit. Curiosity got the better of her.

'Why do you say he's grand?'

'He's at the very top of the tree in the medical world and he's got a Dutch title—comes from an ancient family with lots of money. Never talks about himself. Thomas says he's a very private man.'

'Huh,' said Julia. 'Probably no one's good enough for him.'

Ruth commented mildly, 'You do dislike him, don't you?'

Julia began to wield her scissors again. 'Dislike him? I don't even know him. Shall we have Welsh rarebit for lunch? I'll make some scones for tea. Monica will be ravenous when she gets home; she never has time to eat her sandwiches. And if you're going to the shops you could bring some steak and kidney and I'll make a pudding.' She added, 'Filling and cheap.'

She spoke without rancour; the three Gracey sisters, living together for the sake of economy in the poky little house a long-dead aunt had bequeathed to them, had learned to live frugally. The house might be theirs, but there were rates and taxes, gas and electricity, clothes and food to be paid for. None of them had been trained to do anything in the business world, having been left suddenly with nothing but memories of their mother and father, killed in a car accident, and a carefree life in a pleasant old house in the country with never a thought of money worries.

It had been Julia who'd got them organised, refusing to be daunted by unexpected debts, selling their home to pay off the mortgage, arguing with bank managers, solicitors, and salvaging the remnants of her father's ill-advised investments. Once in their new home, it had been she who had urged the rather shy Ruth to take the part-time job as a receptionist to the local doctor while she looked for work for herself and Monica joined the staff of the local nursery school. But Julia had had no luck until, searching through the ads in the local paper, she'd seen one from the greetings card company.

Nothing ventured, nothing gained, she had decided, and had sat down to compose a batch of verses and send them off. Much to her surprise, the firm had taken her on. It was badly paid, but it meant that she could work at home and do the housekeeping and the cooking. And they managed very well.

Ruth had met Thomas when she had gone to the hospital to collect some urgent path. lab. results for Dr Goodman, and soon they would marry. Monica, although she liked children, had never been quite sure that she wanted to stay at home, especially in such alien surroundings, but then George had come one day to tell the children Bible stories and all ideas of going out into the glamorous world to find a job more to her liking had faded away. They would have to wait to marry, of course, until George had a parish. In the meantime she was happy.

Which left Julia, twenty-four years old, bursting with life and energy. Because she had a happy nature she didn't allow herself to dwell on what might have been, but wrote her sentimental little verses, kept the house clean and tidy and, being clever with her needle, dressed herself in a style which, while not being the height of fashion, was a passable imitation.

It was fortunate, she supposed, that Oscar, her admirer—for he was only that at the moment, although he promised to be rather more when it was convenient for him to be so—had absolutely no taste in clothes. That horrible professor might sneer in a well-mannered way at the curtain, but Oscar wouldn't suspect. Indeed, even if he did, he would probably approve, for he was of a frugal nature when it came to spending money. He was persistent too. She had tried, over and over again, to shake him off, to suggest that she would make him a most unsuitable wife, but he refused to be shaken and, despite the countless excuses she had given, she was committed to attend the annual dance given by the greetings card firm.

Rightly, Ruth and Monica had urged her to go and enjoy herself. But neither of them had met Oscar, and she had given way because she knew that they both felt unhappy at the idea of her being left alone when they married. When she allowed herself to think about it she felt unhappy about that too.

She put away her sewing and started on the household chores, and found herself thinking about the Professor. He seemed a tiresome man, and she suspected that it would be hard to get the better of him. Probably he was horrid to his patients.

Professor van der Maes, contrary to Julia's idea, was treating the endless stream of patients attending his clinic with kindness and patience, his quiet voice reassuring, his smile encouraging. He was a tired man, for he worked too hard, but no patient had ever found him uncaring. But that was a side which he seldom showed to anyone else. The nursing staff who worked for him quickly learnt that he would stand no nonsense, that only their best efforts would suit him, and as for his students—he represented the goal they hoped to obtain one day. A good word from him was worth a dozen from anyone else, just as a quiet reprimand sent them into instant dejection. They called him the old man behind his back, and fiercely defended any criticism anyone was foolish enough to utter.

The Professor remained unmoved by other people's opinion of him, good or bad. He was an excellent surgeon and he loved his work, and he had friends who would be his for life, but he had no use for casual acquaintances. He had a social life when his work permitted, and was much sought after as a dinner party guest. Since he was unmarried, he could have taken his pick of any of the women he met. But, although he was a pleasant companion, he showed no interest in any of them. Somewhere in the world, he supposed, there was the woman he would fall in love with and want for his wife, but he was no longer young and he would probably end his days as a crusty old bachelor.

It wasn't until he was driving back to London a few days later that he thought about the three Gracey sisters. Ruth would make Thomas a good wife: a beautiful girl with her shy smile and gentle voice. He thought only fleetingly of Julia. Pretty, he supposed, but sharp-tongued, and she made no effort to be pleasant. She was the last person he imagined would spend her days writing sentimental verses for greetings cards, and what woman in her senses wore dresses made from curtains? He laughed, and forgot her.

The dance was ten days later, and, since the firm had had a good year, it was to be held at one of the more prestigious hotels. There was to be a buffet supper before everyone went to the hotel ballroom, and Ruth and Monica, anxious that Julia should enjoy herself, lent slippers and an old but still magnificent shawl which had belonged to their mother. They sent her there in a taxi—an unnecessary expense, Julia protested; the journey there would have been a lengthy one by bus but far cheaper. However, they insisted, privately of the opinion that Oscar could have come and fetched her instead of meeting her there...

The dress, despite its origin, was a success, simply made, but it fitted where it should, and unless anyone had actually seen the curtain, hanging in the spare bedroom, one would never have known...

Julia walked out of the taxi feeling quite pleased with herself, straight into the Professor's person.

He set her tidily on her feet. 'Well, well, Miss Julia Gracey. Unexpected and delightful.' He looked around him. 'You are alone?'

She bade him good evening in a choked voice. 'I am meeting someone in the hotel.'

She glanced around, looking without much hope for Oscar. There was no sign of him, of course. He had said that he would be at the hotel entrance, waiting for her. She supposed that she would have to go inside and look for him. She was not easily daunted, but the hotel's imposing entrance and the equally imposing appearance of the doorman daunted her now, and how and by what misfortune had the Professor got here? Surely he hadn't anything to do with greetings cards?

It seemed not. He said easily, 'I'm meeting friends here. We may as well go in together.' He paid the cabby and took her arm. 'Your friend will be looking for you inside?'

He was being kind, with a casual kindness it was impossible to resent. She sought frantically for something to say as the doorman opened the doors with a flourish and they joined the people in the foyer.

There was no sign of Oscar. She had been a fool to accept his invitation; she didn't even like him much.

'Let me have your shawl,' said the Professor. 'I'll let the girl have it.' And he had taken it from her and left her for a moment, returning with a ticket which he tucked into the little handbag hanging from her wrist.

She found her tongue then, 'Thank you. I'll—I'll wait here. Oscar will find me...'

'Oscar?' She mistrusted his casual voice. 'Ah, yes, of course. And if I'm not mistaken this must be he...'

She should have been glad to see him, and she might well have been if he had expressed regret at not meeting her promptly. But all he did was thump her on the shoulder and say heartily, 'Sorry old lady. I got held up; so many people wanted to have a chat.'

He looked her up and down. 'Got yourself a new dress for the occasion? Not bad, not bad at all...'

His glance fell upon the Professor, who had made no attempt to go away.

'Do I know you?'

Julia, aware of the Professor's eyes fixed on the curtain, said tartly, 'No, Oscar, you don't. This is Professor van der Maes. He knows Ruth's fiancé.'

Oscar looked uneasy under the Professor's cool gaze. 'Nice to meet you. Come along, Julia, I'll find you somewhere to sit; I've one or two important clients to talk to, but we'll be able to dance presently.'

He nodded in a condescending manner at the Professor, who took no notice but said pleasantly to Julia, 'I do hope you have a happy evening,' and, as Oscar turned away rudely to speak to a passing cou-

ple, 'but I doubt it.' He looked amused. 'I can't say
that I agree with Oscar about your dress, but then I
know it's a curtain, don't I?'

He was sorry the moment he had said it; for a moment she had the look of a small girl who had been
slapped for no reason at all. But only for a moment.
Julia stared up into his handsome face. 'Go away,
Professor. I don't like you and I hope I never see you
again.'

She had spoken quietly but she looked daggers at
him. She turned her back then, surprised at how upset
she felt. After all, she hadn't liked him the first time,
and she couldn't care less if he jeered at the dress or
liked it. If Oscar liked it, that was all that mattered,
she told herself, not believing a word of it. But presently, when Oscar had finished his conversation, she
went with him to the hotel ballroom, to be sat on one
of the little gilt chairs and told to wait awhile until
he had the leisure to dance with her.

A not very promising prospect—but quickly light-
ened by a number of men who, seeing a pretty girl
sitting by herself, danced her off in rapid succession.
Which served Oscar right by the time he found himself ready to partner her.

'Some of these modern dances are not dignified,'
he told her severely, propelling her round the ballroom with correct stiffness. 'You would have done
better to have sat quietly until I was free to come to
you.'

'But I like to dance, Oscar.'

'Dancing in moderation is splendid exercise,' said
Oscar, at his stuffiest.

They came to a dignified halt as the music stopped.

Julia spoke her thoughts out loud. 'Do you want to marry me, Oscar?' she asked.

He looked at her with astonishment and displeasure.

'My dear Julia, what a very—very...' he sought for the right word '...unwomanly remark to make. I must only hope it was a slight aberration of the tongue.'

'It wasn't anything to do with my tongue; it was a thought in my head.' She looked at him. 'You haven't answered me, Oscar?'

'I have no intention of doing so. I am shocked, Julia. Perhaps you should retire to the ladies' room and compose yourself.'

'You sound like someone in a Victorian novel,' she told him. 'But, yes, I think that would be best.'

The ballroom was at the back of the hotel; it took her a few moments to find the cloakroom where the Professor had left her wrap. She would have to take a bus, she hadn't enough money for a taxi, but it wasn't late and there were plenty of people about. She wrapped the vast mohair shawl she and her sisters shared for evening occasions round her and crossed the foyer, comfortably full of people. And halfway to the door the Professor, apparently appearing from thin air, put a hand on her arm.

'Not leaving already?' he wanted to know. 'It's barely an hour since you arrived.'

She had to stop, his hand, resting so lightly on her arm, nevertheless reminding her of a ball and chain. She said politely, 'Yes, I'm leaving, Professor.' She looked at his hand. 'Goodbye.'

He took no notice; neither did he remove his hand.

'You're upset; you have the look of someone about to explode. I'll take you home.'

'No, thank you. I'm quite capable of getting myself home.'

For answer he tucked her hand under his elbow. 'Your Oscar will come looking for you,' he said mildly.

'He's not my Oscar...'

'Ah, I can't say that I'm surprised. Now, come along. This is indeed a splendid excuse for me to leave with you—a pompous dinner with endless speeches to which I have been bidden.'

He had propelled her gently past the doorman, out into the chilly night and, after towing her along gently, popped her into his car, parked nearby.

Getting in beside her, he asked, 'Are you going to cry?'

'Certainly not. And I have no wish to be here in your car. You are being high-handed, Professor.' She sniffed. 'I'm not a child.'

He looked at her, smiling a little. 'No, I had realised that. Are you hungry?'

She was taken by surprise. 'Yes...'

'Splendid. And, since you are not going to cry and I'm hungry too, we will go and eat somewhere.'

'No,' said Julia.

'My dear girl, be sensible. It's the logical thing to do.' He started the car. 'Let us bury the hatchet for an hour or so. You are free to dislike me the moment I see you to your front door.'

She was hungry, so the prospect of a meal was tempting. She said, 'Well, all right, but not anywhere grand—the curtain...'

He said quietly, 'I'm sorry I said that. You look very nice and it was unforgivable of me. We will go somewhere you won't need to be uneasy.'

He sounded kind and her spirits lifted. Perhaps he wasn't so bad... He spoilt it by adding, 'Is your entire wardrobe made up of curtains?' He glanced at her. 'You must be a very talented young lady.'

She was on the point of making a fiery answer when the thought of a meal crossed her mind. She had no idea why he had asked her out and she didn't care; she would choose all the most expensive things on the menu...

He took her to Wilton's, spoke quietly to the *maître d'*, and followed her to one of the booths, so that any fears concerning her dress were instantly put at rest.

'Now, what shall we have?' asked the Professor, well aware of her relief that the booth sheltered her nicely from the other diners. 'I can recommend the cheese soufflé, and the sole Meunière is excellent.' When she agreed he ordered from the waitress and turned his attention to the *sommelier* and the wine list. Which gave Julia a chance to study the menu. She need not have bothered to choose the most expensive food; everything was expensive.

When it came it was delicious, and cooked by a master hand. She thought fleetingly of Oscar, and applied herself to her dinner, and, being nicely brought up, made polite conversation the while. The Professor replied suitably, amused at that and wondering what had possessed him to take her to dinner. He went out seldom, and when he did his companion would be one of his numerous acquaintances: elegant young women, dressed impeccably, bone-thin and fussing delicately about what they could and couldn't eat.

Julia, on the other hand, ate everything she was offered with an unselfconscious pleasure, and capped the sole with sherry trifle and drank the wine he had ordered. And that loosed her tongue, for presently, over coffee, she asked, 'If you are Dutch, why do you live in England?'

'I only do so for part of the time. My home is in Holland and I work there as well. I shall be going back there in a few weeks' time for a month or so.'

'How very unsettling,' observed Julia. 'But I suppose you are able to pick and choose if you are a Professor?'

'I suppose I can,' he agreed mildly. 'What are you going to do about Oscar?'

'I dare say he won't find me a suitable wife for a junior partner...'

'And will that break your heart?'

'No. He sort of grew on me, if you see what I mean.'

He said smoothly, 'Ah—you have a more romantic outlook, perhaps?'

She took a sip of coffee. 'It's almost midnight. Would you take me home, please?'

Not one of the women he had taken out to dinner had ever suggested that it was getting late and they wished to go home. On the contrary. The Professor stifled a laugh, assured her that they would go at once, and signed the bill. On the journey through London's streets he discussed the weather, the pleasures of the English countryside and the prospect of a fine summer.

The street was quiet and only barely lit. He got out and opened the car door for her, before taking the door key from her. He opened the door and gave her back the key.

Julia cast around in her mind for something gracious to say. 'Thank you for my dinner,' she said finally, and, since that didn't sound in the least gracious, added, 'I enjoyed the dinner very much and the restaurant was—was very elegant. It was a very pleasant evening…'

She didn't like his smile in the dimly lit hallway. 'Don't try too hard, Julia,' he told her. 'Goodnight.'

He pushed her gently into the hall and closed the door soundlessly behind her.

'I hate him,' said Julia, and took off her shoes, flung the shawl onto the floor and crept upstairs to her bed. She had intended to lie awake and consider how much she disliked him, but she went to sleep at once.

The Professor took himself off home, to his elegant Chelsea house, locked the Rolls in the mews garage behind it, and let himself into his home. There was a wall-light casting a gentle light on the side table in the hall and he picked up the handful of letters on it as he went to his study.

This was a small, comfortably furnished room, with rows of bookshelves, a massive desk, a chair behind it and two smaller ones each side of the small fireplace. Under the window was a table with a computer and a pile of papers and books. He ignored it and put the letters on his desk before going out of the room again and along the hall, through the baize door at the end and down the steps to the kitchen, where he poured himself coffee from the pot on the Aga and acknowledged the sleepy greetings from two small dogs.

They got out of the basket they shared and sat beside him while he drank his coffee: two small creatures with heavily whiskered faces, short legs and long, thin rat-like tails. The professor had found them, abandoned, terrified and starving, some six months earlier. It was apparent that they weren't going to grow any larger or handsomer, but they had become members of his household and his devoted companions. He saw them back into their basket, with the promise of a walk in the morning, and went back to his study. There were some notes he needed to write up before he went to bed.

He sat down and pulled the papers towards him and then sat back in his chair, thinking about the evening. What had possessed him to take Julia out to dinner? he wondered. A nice enough girl, no doubt, but with a sharp tongue and making no attempt to hide the fact that she didn't like him. The unknown Oscar was possibly to be pitied. He smiled suddenly. She had enjoyed her dinner, and he doubted whether Oscar rose much above soup of the day and a baked potato. He acknowledged that this was an unfair thought; Oscar might even now be searching fruitlessly for Julia.

When Julia went down to breakfast in the morning, Ruth and Monica were already at the kitchen table, and without wasting time they began to fire questions at her.

'Did you dance? Was it a splendid hotel? What did

you eat? Did Oscar propose? Did he bring you home?'

Julia lifted the teapot. 'I danced three and a half times, and the hotel was magnificent.'

She shook cornflakes into a bowl. She didn't like them, but, according to the TV ad, the girl who ate them had a wand-like figure—a state to which she hoped in time to subdue her own generous curves. She said, 'I didn't eat at the hotel.' She took a sip of tea. 'Oscar didn't propose. I don't think he ever will now. And he didn't bring me home.'

'Julia, you didn't come home alone?'

'No, Professor van der Maes drove me back.'

She finished the cornflakes and put bread in the toaster.

'Start at the beginning and don't leave anything out,' said Ruth. 'What on earth was the Professor doing there? He doesn't write verses, does he?'

'No. Though I'm sure he is very handy with a needle.'

Her sisters exchanged glances. 'Why did you dance half a dance?' asked Ruth.

Julia said through a mouthful of toast, 'Oscar was annoyed because I hadn't stayed on my chair to wait for him, so I asked him if he wanted to marry me.'

'Julia, how could you…?'

'He told me to go to the ladies' room and compose myself, so I found my shawl and left, and the Professor was at the entrance. He said he was hungry and asked me if I was, and when I said yes, he took me to Wilton's.'

'Wilton's?' chorused her sisters, and then added, 'The dress…?'

'It was all right. We sat in a booth. It was a nice dinner. And then, when I asked him to bring me home, he did.'

Two pairs of astonished blue eyes stared at her. 'What about Oscar?'

'He was shocked.'

'And the Professor? Whatever did he say?'

'He said he wasn't surprised that Oscar wasn't mine. You will both be late for work...'

'But why should the Professor take you out to dinner?' asked Ruth.

'He said he was hungry.'

'You can be very tiresome sometimes, Julia,' said Monica severely.

When they had gone Julia set about the household chores and then, those done, she made coffee and a cheese sandwich and sat down to write verses. Perhaps Oscar would be able to get her the sack, but on the other hand her verses sold well. The senior partners might not agree. For it wasn't the kind of work many people would want to do and it was badly paid. She polished off a dozen verses, fed Muffin, the family cat, and peeled the potatoes for supper. Oscar, she reflected, wouldn't bother her again.

CHAPTER TWO

OSCAR came four days later. Julia was making pastry for a steak pie and she went impatiently to the front door when its knocker was thumped. Oscar was on the doorstep. 'I wish to talk to you, Julia.'

'Come in, then,' said Julia briskly. 'I'm making pastry and don't want it to spoil.'

She ushered him into the house, told him to leave his coat in the hall, and then went back into the kitchen and plunged her hands into the bowl.

'Do sit down,' she invited him, and, when he looked askance at Muffin the household cat, sitting in the old Windsor chair by the stove, added, 'Take a chair at the table. It's warm here. Anyway, I haven't lighted the fire in the sitting room yet.'

She bent over her pastry, and presently he said stuffily, 'You can at least leave that and listen to what I have to say, Julia.'

She put the dough on the floured board and held a rolling pin.

'I'm so sorry, Oscar, but I really can't leave it. I am listening, though.'

He settled himself into his chair. 'I have given a good deal of thought to your regrettable behaviour at the dance, Julia. I can but suppose that the excitement of the occasion and the opulence of your surroundings had caused you to become so—so unlike yourself.

After due consideration I have decided that I shall overlook that...'

Julia laid her pastry neatly over the meat and tidied the edges with a knife. 'Don't do that,' she begged him. 'I wasn't in the least excited, only annoyed to be stuck on a chair in a corner—and left to find my own way in, too.'

'I have a position to uphold in the firm,' said Oscar. And when she didn't answer he asked, 'Who was that man you were talking to? Really, Julia, it is most unsuitable. I trust you found your way home? There is a good bus service?'

Julia was cutting pastry leaves to decorate her pie. She said, 'I had dinner at Wilton's and was driven home afterwards.'

Oscar sought for words and, finding none, got to his feet. 'There is nothing more to be said, Julia. I came here prepared to forgive you, but I see now that I have allowed my tolerance to be swept aside by your frivolity.'

Julia dusted her floury hands over the bowl and began to clear up the table. Listening to Oscar was like reading a book written a hundred years ago. He didn't belong in this century and, being a kind-hearted girl, she felt sorry for him.

'I'm not at all suitable for you, Oscar,' she told him gently.

He said nastily, 'Indeed you are not, Julia. You have misled me...'

She was cross again. 'I didn't know we had got to that stage. Anyway, what you need isn't a wife, it's a doormat. And do go, Oscar, before I hit you with this rolling pin.'

He got to his feet. 'I must remind you that your future with the firm is in jeopardy, Julia. I have some influence...'

Which was just what she could have expected from him, she supposed. They went into the hall and he got into his coat. She opened the door and ushered him out, wished him goodbye, and closed the door before he had a chance to say more.

She told her sisters when they came home, and Monica said. 'He might have made a good steady husband, but he sounds a bit out of date.'

'I don't think I want a steady husband,' said Julia, and for a moment she thought about the Professor. She had no idea why she should have done that; she didn't even like him...

So, during the next few days she waited expectantly for a letter from the greetings card firm, but when one did come it contained a cheque for her last batch of verses and a request for her to concentrate on wedding cards—June was the bridal month and they needed to get the cards to the printers in good time...

'Reprieved,' said Julia, before she cashed the cheque and paid the gas bill.

It was difficult to write about June roses and wedded bliss in blustery March. But she wrote her little verses and thought how nice it would be to marry on a bright summer's morning, wearing all the right clothes and with the right bridegroom.

A week later Thomas came one evening. He had got the job as senior registrar and, what was more, had now been offered one of the small houses the hospital rented out to their staff. There was no reason

why he and Ruth shouldn't marry as soon as possible.
The place was furnished, and it was a bit poky, but
once he had some money saved they could find something better.

'And the best of it is I'm working for Professor van
der Maes.' His nice face was alight with the prospect.
'You won't mind a quiet wedding?' he asked Ruth
anxiously.

Ruth would have married him in a cellar wearing
a sack. 'We'll get George to arrange everything. And
it will be quiet anyway; there's only us. Your mother
and father will come?'

Julia went to the kitchen to make coffee and sandwiches and took Monica with her. 'We'll give them
half an hour. Monica, have you any money? Ruth
must have some clothes…'

They sat together at the table, doing sums. 'There
aren't any big bills due,' said Julia. 'If we're very
careful and we use the emergency money we could
just manage.'

Thomas was to take up his new job in three weeks'
time: the best of reasons why he and Ruth should
marry, move into their new home and have a few days
together first. Which meant a special licence and no
time at all to buy clothes and make preparations for
a quiet wedding. Julia and Monica gave Ruth all the
money they could lay hands on and then set about
planning the wedding day. There would be only a
handful of guests: Dr Goodman and his wife, George,
and the vicar who would take the service, Thomas's
parents and the best man.

They got out the best china and polished the teaspoons, and Julia went into the kitchen and leafed through her cookery books.

It was a scramble, but by the time the wedding day dawned Ruth had a dress and jacket in a pale blue, with a fetching hat, handbag, gloves and shoes, and the nucleus of a new wardrobe suitable for a senior registrar's wife. Julia had assembled an elegant buffet for after the ceremony, and Monica had gone to the market and bought daffodils, so that when they reached the church—a red-brick mid-Victorian building, sadly lacking in beauty—its rather bleak interior glowed with colour.

Monica had gone on ahead, leaving Julia to make the last finishing touches to the table, which took longer than she had expected. She had to hurry to the church just as Dr Goodman came for Ruth.

She arrived there a bit flushed, her russet hair glowing under her little green felt hat—Ruth's hat, really, but it went well with her green jacket and skirt, which had been altered and cleaned and altered again and clung to, since they were suitable for serious occasions.

Julia sniffed appreciatively at the fresh scent of the daffodils and started down the aisle to the back views of Thomas and his best man and the sprinkling of people in the pews. It was a long aisle, and she was halfway up when she saw the Professor sitting beside Mrs Goodman. They appeared to be on the best of terms and she shot past their pew without looking at them. His appearance was unexpected, but she supposed that Thomas, now a senior member of the team, merited his presence.

When Ruth came, Julia concentrated on the ceremony, but the Professor's image most annoyingly got between her and the beautiful words of the simple service. There was no need for him to be there. He and Thomas might be on the best of terms professionally, but they surely had different social lives? Did the medical profession enjoy a social life? she wondered, then brought her attention back sharply to Thomas and Ruth, exchanging their vows. They would be happy, she reflected, watching them walk back down the aisle. They were both so sure of their love. She wondered what it must feel like to be so certain.

After the first photos had been taken Julia slipped away, so as to get home before anyone else and make sure that everything was just so.

She was putting the tiny sausage rolls in the oven to warm when Ruth and Thomas arrived, closely followed by everyone else, and presently the best man came into the kitchen to get a corkscrew.

'Not that I think we'll need it,' he told her cheerfully. 'The Prof bought half a dozen bottles of champagne with him. Now that's what I call a wedding gift of the right sort. Can I help?'

'Get everyone drinking. I'll be along with these sausage rolls in a minute or two.'

She had them nicely arranged on a dish when the Professor came into the kitchen. He had a bottle and a glass in one hand.

He said, 'A most happy occasion. Your vicar has had two glasses already.'

He poured the champagne and handed her a glass. 'Thirsty work, heating up sausage rolls.'

She had to laugh. Such light-hearted talk didn't

sound like him at all, and for a moment she liked him. She took her glass and said, 'We can't toast them yet, can we? But it is a happy day.' And, since she was thirsty and excited, she drank deeply.

The Professor had an unexpected feeling of tenderness towards her; she might have a sharp tongue and not like him, but her naïve treatment of a glass of Moet et Chandon Brut Imperial he found touching.

She emptied the glass and said, 'That was nice.'

He agreed gravely. 'A splendid drink for such an occasion,' and he refilled her glass, observing prudently, 'I'll take the tray in for you.'

The champagne was having an effect upon her empty insides. She gave him a wide smile. 'The best man—what's his name, Peter?—said he'd be back...'

'He will be refilling glasses.' The Professor picked up the tray, opened the door and ushered her out of the kitchen.

Julia swanned around, light-headed and light-hearted. It was marvellous what a couple of glasses of champagne did to one. She ate a sausage roll, drank another glass of champagne, handed round the sandwiches and would have had another glass of champagne if the Professor hadn't taken the glass from her.

'They're going to cut the cake,' he told her, 'and then we'll toast the happy couple.' Only then did he hand her back her glass.

After Ruth and Thomas had driven away, and everyone else was going home, she realised that the Professor had gone too, taking the best man with him.

'He asked me to say goodbye,' said Monica as the pair of them sat at the kitchen table, their shoes off, drinking strong tea. 'He took the best man with him, said he was rather pressed for time.'

Julia, still pleasantly muzzy from the champagne, wondered why it was that the best man had had the time to say goodbye to her. If he'd gone with the Professor, then surely the Professor could have found the time to do the same? She would think about that when her head was a little clearer.

Life had to be reorganised now that Ruth had left home; they missed her share of the housekeeping, but by dint of economising they managed very well.

Until, a few weeks later, Monica came into the house like a whirlwind, calling to Julia to come quickly; she had news.

George had been offered a parish; a small rural town in the West country. 'Miles from anywhere,' said Monica, glowing with happiness, 'but thriving. Not more than a large village, I suppose, but very scattered. He's to go there this week and see if he likes it.'

'And if he does?'

'He'll go there in two weeks' time. I'll go with him, of course. We can get married by special licence first.' Then she danced round the room. 'Oh, Julia, isn't it all marvellous? I'm so happy…!'

It wasn't until later, after they had toasted the future in a bottle of wine from the supermarket, that Monica said worriedly, 'Julia, what about you? What will you do? You'll never be able to manage…'

Julia had had time to have an answer ready. She said cheerfully, 'I shall take in lodgers until we decide what to do about this house. You and Ruth will probably like to sell it, and I think that is a good thing.'

'But you?' persisted Monica.

'I shall go to dressmaking classes and then set up on my own. I shall like that.'

'You don't think Oscar will come back? If he really loved you...?'

'But he didn't, and I wouldn't go near him with a bargepole— whatever that means.'

'But you'll marry...?'

'Oh, I expect so. And think how pleased my husband will be to have a wife who makes her own clothes.'

Julia poured the last of the wine into their glasses. 'Now tell me your plans...'

She listened to her sister's excited voice, making suitable comments from time to time, making suggestions, and all the while refusing to give way to the feeling of panic. So silly, she told herself sternly; she had a roof over her head for the time being, and she was perfectly able to reorganise her life. She wouldn't be lonely; she would have lodgers and Muffin...

'You'll marry from here?' she asked.

'Yes, but very quietly. We'll go straight to the parish after the wedding. There'll be just us and Ruth— and Thomas, if he can get away. No wedding breakfast or anything.' Monica laughed. 'I always wanted a big wedding, you know—white chiffon and a veil and bridesmaids—but none of that matters. It'll have to be early in the morning.'

Monica's lovely face glowed with happiness, and Julia said, 'Aren't you dying to hear what the vicarage is like? And the little town? You'll be a marvellous vicar's wife.'

'Yes, I think I shall,' said Monica complacently.

Presently she said uncertainly, 'Are you sure you'll be all right, Julia? There has always been the three of us...'

'Of course I'll be fine—and how super that I'll be able to visit you. Once I get started I can get a little car...'

Which was daydreaming with a vengeance, but served to pacify Monica.

After that events crowded upon each other at a great rate. George found his new appointment very much to his liking; moreover, he had been accepted by the church wardens and those of the parish whom he had met with every sign of satisfaction. The vicarage was large and old-fashioned, but there was a lovely garden... He was indeed to take up his appointment in two weeks' time, which gave them just that time to arrange their wedding—a very quiet one, quieter even than Ruth's and Thomas's, for they were to marry in the early morning and drive straight down to their new home.

Julia, helping Monica to pack, had little time to think about anything else, but was relieved that the girl who was to take over Monica's job had rented a room with her: a good omen for the future, she told her sisters cheerfully. Trudie seemed a nice girl, too, quiet and studious, and it would be nice to have someone else in the house, and nicer still to have the rent money...

She would have to find another lodger, thought Julia, waving goodbye to George's elderly car and the newly married pair. If she could let two rooms she would be able to manage if she added the rent to the small amounts she got from the greetings card firm. Later on, she quite understood, Ruth and Monica would want to sell the house, and with her own share she would start some kind of a career...

She went back into the empty house; Trudie would be moving in on the following morning and she must make sure that her room was as welcoming as possible. As soon as she had a second lodger and things were running smoothly, she would pay a visit to Ruth.

A week went by. It was disappointing that there had been no replies to her advertisement; she would have to try again in a week or so, and put cards in the windows of the row of rather seedy shops a few streets away. In the meantime she would double her output of verses.

Trudie had settled in nicely, coming and going quietly, letting herself in and out with the key Julia had given her. Another one like her would be ideal, reflected Julia, picking up the post from the doormat.

There was a letter from the greetings card firm and she opened it quickly; there would be a cheque inside. There was, but there was a letter too. The firm was changing its policy: in future they would deal only with cards of a humorous nature since that was what the market demanded. It was with regret that they would no longer be able to accept her work. If she had a batch ready to send then they would accept it, but nothing further.

Julia read the letter again, just to make sure, and then went into the kitchen, made a pot of tea and sat down to drink it. It was a blow; the money the firm paid her was very little but it had been a small, steady income. Its loss would be felt. She did some sums on the back of the envelope and felt the beginnings of a headache. It was possible that Oscar was behind it... She read the letter once again; they would accept one last batch. Good, she would send as many verses as she could think up. She got pencil and paper and set to work. Just let me say on this lovely day...she began, and by lunchtime had more than doubled her output.

She typed them all out on her old portable and took them to the post. It would have been satisfying to have torn up the letter and put it in an envelope and sent it back, but another cheque would be satisfying too.

The cheque came a few days later, but still no new lodger. Which, as it turned out, was a good thing...

Thomas phoned. Ruth was in bed with flu, could she possibly help out for a day or two? Not to stay, of course, but an hour or two each day until Ruth was on her feet. There was a bus, he added hopefully.

It meant two buses; she would have to change halfway. The hospital wasn't all that far away, but was awkward to get to.

Julia glanced at the clock. 'I'll be there about lunchtime. I must tell Trudie, my lodger. I'll stay until the evening if that's OK.'

'Bless you,' said Thomas. 'I should be free about five o'clock.'

Trudie, summoned from a horde of toddlers, was helpful. She would see to Muffin, go back at lunchtime and make sure that everything was all right, and she wasn't going out that evening anyway. Julia hurried to the main street and caught a bus.

The house was close to the hospital, one of a neat row in which the luckier of the medical staff lived. The door key, Thomas had warned her, was under the pot of flowers by the back door, and Julia let herself in, calling out as she did so.

It was a very small house. She put her bag down in the narrow hall and went up the stairs at its end, guided by the sound of Ruth's voice.

She was propped up in bed, her lovely face only slightly dimmed by a red nose and puffy eyes. She said thickly, 'Julia, you darling. You don't mind coming? I feel so awful, and Thomas has to be in Theatre all day. I'll be better tomorrow…'

'You'll stay there until Thomas says that you can get up,' said Julia, 'and of course I don't mind coming. In fact it makes a nice change. Now, how about a wash and a clean nightie, and then a morsel of something to eat?'

'I hope you don't catch the flu,' said Ruth later, drinking tea and looking better already, drowsy now in her freshly made bed, her golden hair, though rather lank, it must be admitted, neatly brushed. All the same, thought Julia, she looked far from well.

'Has the doctor been?' she asked.

'Yes, Dr Soames, one of the medical consultants. Someone is coming with some pills…'

Thomas brought them during his lunch hour. He couldn't stop, his lunch 'hour' being a figure of speech. A cup of coffee and a sandwich was the norm on this day, when Professor van der Maes was operating, but he lingered with Ruth as long as he could, thanked Julia profusely and assured her that he would be back by five o'clock. 'I'll be on call,' he told her, 'but only until midnight.'

'Would you like me to keep popping in for a few days, until Ruth is feeling better?'

'Would you? I hate leaving her.'

He went then, and Julia went down to the little kitchen, made another hot drink for Ruth and boiled herself an egg. Tomorrow she would bring some fruit and a new loaf. Bread and butter, cut very thin, was something most invalids would eat.

It was almost six o'clock when Thomas returned, bringing the Professor with him. The Professor spent a few minutes with Ruth, assured Thomas that she was looking better, and wandered into the kitchen, where Julia was laying a tray of suitable nourishment for Ruth.

'Get your coat,' he told her. 'I'll drive you home.'

Julia thumped a saucepan of milk onto the stove. 'Thank you, but I'll get a bus when I'm ready.'

Not so much as a hello or even a good evening, thought Julia pettishly.

His smile mocked her. 'Thomas is here now. Two's company, three's none.'

'Thomas will want his supper.'

Thomas breezed into the kitchen. 'I'm a first-rate cook. We're going to have a picnic upstairs. You go home, Julia. You've been a godsend, and we're so grateful. You will come tomorrow?'

'Yes,' said Julia, and without looking at either of the men went and got her coat, said goodnight to her sister and went downstairs again.

The two men were in the hall and Thomas backed

into the open kitchen door to make room for her, but even then the professor took up almost all the space. He opened the door and she squeezed past him into the street. Thomas came too, beaming at them both, just as though he was seeing them off for an evening out.

The Professor had nothing to say. He sat relaxed behind the wheel, and if he felt impatience at the heavy traffic he didn't show it. Watching the crowded pavements and the packed buses edging their way along the streets, Julia suddenly felt ashamed at her ingratitude.

'This is very kind of you,' she began. 'It would have taken me ages to get home.'

He said coolly, 'I shan't be going out of my way. I'm going to the children's hospital not five minutes' drive away from your home.'

A remark which hardly encouraged her to carry on the conversation.

He had nothing more to say then, but when he stopped before her house he got out, opened the car door for her and stood waiting while she unlocked the house door, dismissing her thanks with a laconic, 'I have already said it was no trouble. Goodnight, Julia.'

She stood in the open door as he got into the car and drove off.

'And that's the last time I'll accept a lift from you,' she said to the empty street. 'I can't think why you bothered, but I suppose Thomas was there and you had no choice.' She slammed the door. 'Horrid man.'

But she was aware of a kind of sadness; she was sure that he wasn't a horrid man, only where she was concerned. For some reason she annoyed him...

She got her supper, fed Muffin, and went to warn Trudie that she would be going to Ruth for the next few days. 'No one phoned about a room, I suppose?' she asked.

'Not a soul. Probably in a day or two you'll have any number of callers.'

But there was no one.

For the next few days Julia went to and fro while Ruth slowly improved. Of the Professor there was no sign, although her sister told her that he had come frequently to see her. Dr Soames came too, and told her that she was much better. 'Though I look a hag,' said Ruth.

'A beautiful hag,' said Julia bracingly, 'and tomorrow you're going to crawl downstairs for a couple of hours.'

Ruth brightened. 'Tom can get the supper and we'll have it round the fire, and I dare say Gerard will come for an hour...'

'Gerard?'

'The Professor. I simply couldn't go on calling him Professor, even though he seems a bit staid and stand-offish, doesn't he? But he's not in the least, and he's only thirty-six. He ought to be married, he nearly was a year ago, but he's not interested in girls. Not to marry, anyway. He's got lots of friends, but they're just friends.'

'You surprise me...'

Ruth gave her a thoughtful look. 'You don't like him?'

'I don't know him well enough to know if I like or dislike him.'

Ruth gave her a sharp look. 'I'm feeling so much

better; I'm sure I could manage. You've been an angel, coming each day, but you must be longing to be let off the hook.'

'There's nothing to keep me at home. Trudie looks after herself and keeps an eye on Muffin. And if you can put up with me for another few days I think it might be a good idea.'

'Oh, darling, would you really come? Just for a couple more days. I do feel so much better, but not quite me yet...'

'Of course I'll come. And we'll see how you are in two days' time.'

After those two days Julia had to admit that Ruth was quite able to cope without any help from her. It was all very well for her to spend the day there while Ruth was in bed, but now that she was up—still rather wan—Julia felt that Ruth and Tom would much rather be on their own.

The moment she arrived the next morning she told Ruth briskly, 'This is my last day; you don't need me any more...'

Ruth was sitting at the table in the tiny kitchen, chopping vegetables. She looked up, laughing. 'Oh, but I do. Sit down and I'll tell you.'

Julia took a bite of carrot. 'You want me to make curtains for the bathroom? I told you everyone could see in if they tried hard enough.'

'Curtains, pooh! Dr Soames says I need a little holiday, and Thomas says so too. He wants you to go with me. Do say you can. You haven't got another lodger yet, and Trudie could look after Muffin.'

'You're going to Monica's?' It would be lovely to

go away from the dull little house and duller street. 'Yes, of course I'll come.'

'You will? You really won't mind? Thomas won't let me go alone...' She added quickly, 'And we're not going to Monica. We're going to Holland.'

Before Julia could speak, she added, 'Gerard has a little cottage near a lake. There's no one there, only his housekeeper. He says it's very quiet there, and the country's pretty and just what I need. Thomas wants me to go. He's got a couple of days due to him and he'll drive us there.'

'There won't be anyone else there? Only us?'

'Yes, you and I. Tom will stay one night and come and fetch us back—he won't know exactly when, but it will be a week or two. You're not having second thoughts?'

Which was exactly what Julia was having, but one look at her sister's still pale face sent them flying; Ruth needed to get away from London and a week in the country would get her back onto her feet again. Although early summer so far had been chilly and wet, there was always the chance that it would become warm and sunny. She said again, 'Of course I'll love to come. I'll fix things up with Trudie. When are we to go?'

'Well, Thomas can get Saturday and Sunday off— that's in three days' time. We shan't need many clothes, so you'll only need to bring a case—and I've enough money for both of us.'

'Oh, I've plenty of money,' said Julia, with such an air of conviction that she believed it herself.

'You have? Well, I suppose you have more time to

work for the greetings card people now, and of course there's the rent from Trudie...'

Which was swallowed up almost before Julia had put it into her purse. But Ruth didn't have to know that, and she certainly wasn't going to tell anyone that she no longer had a market for her little verses. There would be another lodger soon, she told herself bracingly and she would find a part-time job; in the meantime she would enjoy her holiday.

The nagging thought that it was the Professor who had been the means of her having one rankled all the way home. For some reason she hated to be beholden to him.

She felt better about that when she came to the conclusion that he didn't know that she would be going; beyond offering the use of his house, he wouldn't be concerned with the details.

The Professor, phoning instructions to his housekeeper in Holland, was very well aware that she would be going with Ruth; he had himself suggested it, with just the right amount of casualness. He wasn't sure why he had done so but he suspected that he had wanted her to feel beholden to him.

He was an aloof man by nature, and an unhappy love affair had left him with a poor opinion of women. There were exceptions: his own family, his devoted housekeeper, his elderly nanny, the nursing staff who worked for him, life-long friends, wives of men he had known for years. He had added Ruth to the list, so in love with her Thomas—and so different from her sharp-tongued sister. And yet—there was something about Julia...

*   *   *

No need to take a lot of clothes, Ruth had said. Julia foraged through her wardrobe and found a leaf-brown tweed jacket, so old that it was almost fashionable once again. There was a pleated skirt which went quite well with it, a handful of tops and a jersey dress. It was, after all, getting warmer each day. As it was country they would go walking, she supposed, so that meant comfortable shoes. She could travel in the new pair she had had for the weddings. She added undies, a scarf and a thin dressing gown, and then sat down to count her money. And that didn't take long! There would be a week's rent from Trudie to add, and when she got back there would be another lot waiting for her. She went in search of her lodger and enlisted her help.

Trudie was a quiet, unassuming girl, saving to get married, good-natured and trustworthy. She willingly agreed to look after Muffin and make sure that the house was locked up at night.

'You could do with a holiday. No doubt when you get back you'll have a house full of lodgers and not a moment to yourself.'

A prospect which should have pleased Julia but somehow didn't.

Three days later Thomas and Ruth came to fetch her. They were to go by the catamaran from Harwich, a fast sea route which would get them to their destination during the afternoon. Julia, who had received only a garbled version of where they were going, spent a great part of their journey studying a map— a large, detailed one which the Professor had thoughtfully provided.

Somewhere south of Amsterdam and not too far

from Hilversum. And there were any number of lakes and no large towns until one reached Utrecht.

Ruth said over her shoulder, 'It's really country, Julia. Gerard says we don't need to go near a town unless we want to, although it's such a small country there are lots of rural areas with only tiny villages.'

It didn't seem very rural when they landed at the Hoek and took to the motorway, for small towns followed each other in quick succession, but then Thomas turned into a minor road and Julia saw the Holland she had always pictured. Wide landscapes, villages encircling churches much too large for them, farms with vast barns and water meadows where cows wandered. And the further they drove the more remote it became. The land was flat, but now there were small copses and glimpses of water. Julia looked around her and sighed with pleasure. Maybe there were large towns nearby, and main roads, but here there was an age-old peace and quiet.

Ruth, who had been chattering excitedly, had fallen silent and Thomas said, 'See that church spire beyond those trees? Unless I've read the map wrongly, we're here...'

CHAPTER THREE

WHEN they reached the trees Thomas turned into a narrow brick lane between them which opened almost at once into a scattered circle of houses grouped around the church. Any of the houses would do, thought Julia, for they were really all cottages, some larger than others, all with pristine paintwork, their little windows sparkling. But Thomas encircled the church and went along a narrow lane, leading away from the road.

'Hope I'm right,' he said. 'The Prof said it was easy to find, but of course he lives here! Five hundred yards past the church on the right-hand side...'

They all chorused 'There it is,' a moment later. It was another cottage, but a good deal larger than those in the village, with a wide gate and a short drive leading to the front door.

It had a red-tiled roof, white walls and small windows arranged precisely on either side of its solid door, and it was set in a garden glowing with flowers, all crammed together in a glorious mass of colour. Julia, standing by the car, rotated slowly, taking it all in. She hadn't been sure what kind of a house the Professor would have—something dignified and austerely perfect, she had supposed, because that would have reflected him. But this little cottage—and not so little now that she had had a good look—was definitely cosy, its prettiness fit to grace the most sentimental of greetings cards. She tried to imagine him in his impeccable grey suiting, mowing the lawn…!

The door had been opened and a short, stout lady surged to meet them.

She was talking before she reached them. 'There you are—come on in. You must want a cup of tea, and I made some scones.'

She shook hands all round, beaming at them. 'Mrs Beckett, the housekeeper, and delighted to welcome you. Such a nice day you've had for travelling, and it's to be hoped that we'll get some fine weather. A bit of sun and fresh air will soon put you back on your feet, Mrs Scott.'

She had urged them indoors as she spoke. 'Now, just you make yourselves comfortable for a minute while I fetch the tea tray, then you can see your rooms. A pity Mr Scott can't stay longer, but there, you're a busy man like Mr Gerard. Always on the go, he is, pops in to see me whenever he can, bless him. He's so good to his old nanny.'

She paused for breath, said, 'Tea', and trotted out of the room.

Thomas sat Ruth down in one of the small armchairs and went to look out of the window. Ruth said, 'Oh, darling, isn't this heavenly? I'm going to love it here, only I'm going to miss you.'

Thomas went and sat beside her, and Julia wandered round inspecting the room. It was low-ceilinged, with rugs on the wooden floor, comfortable chairs and small tables scattered around a fireplace with a wood stove flanked by bookshelves bulging with books. Julia heaved a sigh of contentment and turned round as Mrs Beckett came in with the tea tray.

They were taken round the cottage presently—first to the kitchen, with its flagstone floor and scrubbed table and old-fashioned dresser, its rows of saucepans on either side of the Aga and comfortable Windsor chairs on either side of it. And on each chair a cat.

'Portly and Lofty,' said Mrs Beckett. 'Keep me company, they do. Mr Gerard brought them here years ago—kittens they were then; he'd found them.'

She led the way out of the kitchen. 'There's a cloakroom here, and that door is his study, and there's a garden room...'

Upstairs there were several bedrooms, and two bathrooms luxurious enough to grace the finest of houses.

'He does himself proud,' murmured Julia, leaning out of the window of the room which was to be hers.

They strolled round the garden presently, and then Julia went to her room again on the pretext of unpacking, but really so that Thomas and Ruth could be together. And later, after a delicious meal of asparagus, lamb cutlets, new potatoes and baby carrots, followed by caramel custard and all washed down by a crisp white wine, she excused herself from taking an evening stroll with the other two on the plea of tiredness. Not that she was in the least tired. She slept soundly, waking early to lie in bed examining the room.

It wasn't large, but whoever had chosen the furniture had known exactly what was right for it: there was a mahogany bed with a rose-patterned quilt and a plump pink eiderdown, pale rugs on the polished floor, a small dressing table under the window and a crinoline chair beside a small table. There were flowers on the table in a Delft bowl.

Like a fairy tale, decided Julia, and got up to lean out of the window.

Mrs Beckett's voice begging her to get back into bed and not catch cold sent her back under the eiderdown to drink the tea offered her.

Breakfast would be in half an hour, said Mrs Beckett, sounding just as an old-fashioned nanny would sound. 'Porridge and scrambled eggs, for I can see that Mrs Scott needs feeding up.' Her small twinkling eyes took in Julia's splendid shape. 'Women should look like women,' observed Mrs Beckett.

I shall get fat, thought Julia, buttering her third piece of toast. Not that it mattered. Now, if she were married to someone like Thomas she would go on a diet; men, so the TV advertisements proclaimed with such certainty, liked girls with wand-like shapes...

Declaring that she wanted postcards, she took herself off to the village and didn't get back until lunchtime. Thomas was to leave shortly and Ruth did most of the talking: clean shirts, and mind to remember to change his socks, and to wind the kitchen clock, and she hoped that she had stocked the fridge with enough food...

'I'll be back in just over a week, darling,' said Thomas.

When he had gone Mrs Beckett sent them to the village again, to buy rolls and croissants for breakfast, and they strolled back while Ruth speculated as to Thomas's progress. Julia put in a sympathetic word here and there and ate one of the rolls, still warm from the bakery.

'You'll get fat,' said Ruth.

'Who cares?' The strong wish that someone would care kept her silent; it would be very nice if someone—someone who didn't even like her very much, like the Professor—would actually look at her and care enough to discourage her from eating rolls warm from the oven.

There was no reason why she should think of him, she told herself. It was because she was staying at his home, and it was difficult to forget that. I don't like him anyway, she reminded herself.

Between them, she and Mrs Beckett set about getting Ruth quite well again. It was surprising what a few days of good food, temptingly cooked, walks in the surrounding countryside and sound sleep did for her. After five days Ruth satisfied her two companions; she was now pink-cheeked and bright-eyed and, although she missed Thomas, she was willing to join in any plans Julia might suggest.

Another four or five days, thought Julia, getting up early because it was such a lovely morning, and we shall be going home again. But she wouldn't spoil the day by thinking about that. She skipped downstairs and out of the front door.

The Professor was sitting on the low stone wall beside the door. He didn't look like the Professor; the elderly trousers and a turtle-necked sweater had wiped years off him. He said, 'Hello, Julia,' and smiled.

She stood staring, and then said, 'How did you get here? It's not eight o'clock yet.' A sudden thought struck her. 'Is Thomas ill? Is something wrong?'

'So many questions and you haven't even wished me good morning. Thomas is in the best of health;

nothing is wrong. I came to make sure that you were both comfortable here.'

'Comfortable? It's heaven! How did you get here?'

'I flew.''

'You flew? But how? I mean, do planes fly so early in the morning?'

'I have my own plane.'

'Your own plane?'

'This conversation is getting repetitive, Julia.'

'Yes, well, I'm surprised. Are you going to stay?'

'Don't worry, only for an hour or so.'

'And you'll fly back? You mean to say you've come just for an hour or so?' The Professor smiled, and she hopped onto the wall beside him. 'When we got here I was surprised—it didn't seem your kind of home. But now you're in slacks and a sweater I can see that it is. I just couldn't picture you in grey worsted and gold cufflinks being here…'

He didn't allow his amusement to show. 'You make me feel middle-aged.'

'Oh, no. Ruth told me that you're thirty-six or so, but you're remote, indifferent…' She paused to look at him. He was smiling again, but this time it was a nasty smile which sent her to her feet. 'I'll tell Ruth you're here.'

Indoors, flying up the stairs, her cheeks burning, she wondered what on earth had possessed her to talk to him like that. It was because he had seemed different, she supposed, but he wasn't, only his clothes. He was still a man she didn't like. She would make some excuse to go to the village after breakfast and stay there until he had gone again.

When, at the end of the meal, she stated her inten-

tions, he told her carelessly to enjoy her walk, while
Ruth said, 'Get me some more cards if you go to the
shop, Julia.'

Mrs Beckett observed, 'You'd best say goodbye to
Mr Gerard; he'll be gone before you get back.'

So Julia wished him goodbye, and he got up and
opened the door for her—a courtesy which she was
convinced was as false as his friendly, 'Goodbye,
Julia.'

She spent a long time in the village—buying things
she didn't need, going the long way back, loitering
through the garden—for he might still be there.

He wasn't. 'How kind of him to come and make
sure we were all right,' said Ruth. 'And he's arranging things so that Thomas can spend the night here
before we go back next week. I've loved being here,
but I do miss Tom...'

She glanced at Julia. 'You haven't been bored? We
haven't gone anywhere or done anything or met anyone...'

Julia was replaiting her tawny hair. A pity she
hadn't put it up properly with pins that morning; a
pigtail over one shoulder lacked dignity.

'I've loved every minute of it,' Well, this morning
was something best forgotten. It was obvious that the
Professor had no intention of being friendly—something which she found upsetting and that considering
she didn't like him in the least, was puzzling. All the
same, just for a little while she had enjoyed sitting
there on the wall beside him.

It had turned warm, warm enough to sit in the garden or potter around watching things grow. She
would have liked to have weeded and raked and

pulled the rhubarb and grubbed up radishes and lettuce from the kitchen garden at the back of the house, but the dour old man in charge wouldn't allow that. Whatever the language, it was obvious he objected strongly to anyone so much as laying a finger on a blade of grass.

Thomas phoned each day. The professor had arrived back safely, he told Ruth, and had gone straight to his late-afternoon clinic. News which Julia received without comment and an inward astonishment at the man's energy.

The week passed too quickly. Thomas would come on Saturday morning, so they must be ready to leave soon after breakfast. Julia, packing her few things, looked round her charming room with real regret; she was going to miss the comfort and unobtrusive luxury of the cottage, and still more she would miss Mrs Beckett's company. She was a contented soul, only wanting everyone else to be contented—the kind of person one could confide in, reflected Julia, who had, in truth, told her a good deal about her hopes and plans. And quite unwittingly revealed her uncertainty as to the future.

Mrs Beckett had listened with real sympathy and some sound advice. It wouldn't be needed, of course; if ever two people were made for each other they were Julia and Mr Gerard. Of course, they hadn't discovered that yet, but time would tell, reflected Mrs Beckett comfortably.

The sun shone on Saturday morning, and the garden had never looked so lovely. Julia, dressed and ready to leave, had gone into the garden to wish it goodbye. Ruth was in the kitchen with Mrs Beckett, but Julia didn't want to wish her goodbye until the very last minute. She strolled round, sniffing at the flowers and shrubs, and, coming upon a patch of white violets, got down on her knees to enjoy their scent.

'My mother planted those,' said the Professor from behind her.

Julia shot to her feet in shock and whirled round. 'Why are you here again?' she demanded.

'This is my home,' he said mildly.

Julia went red. 'I'm sorry, that was rude, but you took me by surprise.'

When he didn't speak she added, 'Have you come to stay? We are so grateful to you for inviting us to stay here. We've had a glorious time. You must be very happy living here; the garden is so beautiful too.'

'What a polite little speech.' The faint mockery in his voice brought the colour back into her cheeks once more. 'I'm glad that you have enjoyed your stay. Are you ready to leave? Mrs Beckett will have coffee waiting for us.'

She went into the house with him, not speaking, and Ruth came running to meet them.

'Julia, isn't it wonderful? Thomas can stay until tomorrow. We're going to fly back—we shall have a whole day together.' She put a hand on the Professor's sleeve. 'You've been so kind...'

'Thomas is due a couple of days off, and this has given me a good excuse to arrange things to suit all of us. I'm only sorry I can't stay longer.'

He took the mug of coffee Mrs Beckett offered him. 'I'll see Julia safely home.'

She was swallowing hot coffee...choked, and had

to suffer the indignity of having her back patted and being mopped up. Then she said frostily, 'Is this something I should know about?'

Ruth laughed. 'Oh, didn't the Professor tell you? He's driving you back.' Before Julia could utter, he said, 'We need to leave in five minutes or so. I've patients to see later on today.'

Julia said childishly, 'But you've only just got here. I'm sure you must want to stay.'

'Indeed I do. As it is, I can't. So, if you would do whatever you still need to do, we'll be on our way.'

They were all looking at her and smiling; the Professor's smile was brief and amused and he turned away to stroll to the window and study the garden. She fetched her jacket, and was kissed and hugged and escorted to the Rolls with exclamations of delight at her good fortune at having such a comfortable journey.

Ruth poked her head through the window. 'I'll phone you when we get back. Trudie will be there, won't she? You won't be alone?'

'Who is Trudie?' asked the Professor as she settled back after a last wave.

'My lodger. Which way are you going back?'

'From Calais by hovercraft. That should get us back by the late afternoon.'

She must make an effort to be an agreeable companion—probably he didn't want her company anymore than she wanted his. 'A long drive,' she observed, striving for an easy friendliness.

It was at once doused by his casual, 'Yes—doze off if you want to, and you have no need to make polite small talk.'

Rude words bubbled and died on her lips; she couldn't utter them; he was giving her a lift, and she depended on him until she was back on her own doorstep. She sat silently seething, staring out at the countryside. But once they had reached the motorway there wasn't a great deal to look at, only the blue and white signposts at regular intervals. She watched them flash past.

'Why are we going to Amsterdam?' she wanted to know. 'You said we were going to Calais; you ought to be going south.'

He answered her in a patient voice which set her teeth on edge. 'We are going to Amsterdam because I need to. From there we will continue on our way to Calais. Don't worry, we are in plenty of time to catch the ferry.'

'I'm not worried.' Since there was nothing more to be said, she lapsed once more into silence.

But once they reached the city and had driven through its suburbs and reached the heart of it she forgot to be quiet. The old streets were lovely, the houses lining them much as they had been three hundred years earlier. 'Look at that canal,' she begged him, 'and those dear little bridges—and there's a barge simply loaded with flowers—and I can hear bells ringing...'

'Carillons. The barge is moored close to the street so that people can buy the flowers if they wish. There are bridges everywhere connecting up the streets. We are going over the one you see ahead of us.'

The street on the other side of it was narrow, brick-built and lined with large gabled houses on one side and a narrow canal on the other side.

Halfway down it the professor stopped the car, got out and opened her door.

'Would you rather I stayed in the car?' asked Julia. 'Perhaps…'

He opened the car door wider. 'Come along, I haven't time to waste.'

She got out huffily then, and went wordlessly with him up the double steps to the solid front door with its ornate transom. She was hating every minute of it, she told herself, while admitting to a longing to see inside the house. Friends of his, she wondered, or some kind of business to do with his work?

The rather bent elderly man who opened the door broke into voluble Dutch at the sight of them, which was of no help at all. It was obvious that he knew the Professor, and that the Professor held him in some regard, for he had clapped him gently on the back as they went in and addressed him at some length.

She allowed her gaze to wander around their surroundings and felt a surge of pleasure. They were in a long narrow hall with doors on either side and at its end a curving staircase. The walls were panelled, and it was all rather dark, but it was sombrely rich, she told herself, with a brass chandelier, undoubtedly old, a black and white tiled floor strewn with rugs of colours faded with age and a console table upon which someone had set a porcelain bowl of flowers.

The Professor's voice recalled her to her surroundings.

'This is Wim. He looks after the house and everyone in it.' When she offered a hand it was gently shaken and she was made welcome in his thin reedy voice.

The penny dropped then. 'This is your house?' said Julia.

'Yes. My home. We will have coffee and then I must ask you to excuse me while I deal with one or two matters. We must leave in half an hour or so.'

Wim was going ahead of them to open a door, into a long narrow room, panelled, like the hall, and furnished with comfortable chairs grouped round a vast fireplace. Its walls were lined with cabinets, a great long-case clock and a walnut bureau bookcase. There were small tables too, bearing gently shaded lamps, their glow enough, with the firelight, to bathe the room in soft light. And the room had an occupant, for a large dog came bounding to meet them, large and woolly with fearsome teeth.

'It's all right; he's only smiling,' said the professor, bracing himself to receive the delighted onslaught of the devoted beast.

'This is Jason, he's a Bouvier, a splendid chap who will guard those he loves with his life. Offer him a fist.'

Julia liked dogs, but she tried not to see the teeth as she did as she was told—to have her hand gently licked while small yellow eyes studied her face from under a tangle of hair. She said, 'I'm Julia,' and patted the woolly head.

'You must miss him,' she said, and sat down in the chair the Professor was offering.

'Yes, but I plan to spend more time here than in England. In the meantime, I snatch a few moments whenever I can.'

A casual remark which left her feeling vaguely disquiet.

Wim came in with coffee, and presently the Professor excused himself on the grounds of phone calls to make.

'We must leave in fifteen minutes. Wim will show you where you can tidy yourself.'

He went away, Jason at his heels, and Julia was left to finish her coffee before going slowly round the room, inspecting its treasures. She supposed that it was the drawing room, but there were several other doors in the hall. It was a large house; if all its rooms were as splendidly furnished as this one then the Professor must live in some style.

'Ancestors going back for ever and ever,' said Julia, addressing a portrait of a forbidding gentleman in a wig, 'and loaded with money.'

She became aware of a wet tongue on her hand. Jason was standing silently beside her. She turned quickly; the Professor would have heard her... But apparently he hadn't; he was across the room, looking out of a window. She sighed with relief and said quickly, 'You want to go? If I could ask Wim...?'

'By the staircase. The door on the right. Don't be long.'

He sounded much the same as usual: polite, detached, faintly amused. She joined him after a few minutes with the polite remark that she hoped she hadn't kept him waiting, bade goodbye to Wim and was swept out to the car without any further delay. Jason, standing in the hall, had rumbled goodbye when she had bent to stroke him, and on impulse she had bent down and thrown her arms around his neck and hugged him.

'You mustn't mind,' she'd said softly. 'He'll be back soon.'

She had turned away then, not wanting to see the parting between master and dog.

The Professor drove through the city and onto the motorway, giving her little opportunity to look around her. She sat silently beside him, sensing that he didn't wish to talk. No doubt he had a great many important matters to think about. She settled down to watch the countryside. He was driving fast and she was enjoying the speed; it was a pity that the motorway bypassed the villages and towns, but there was plenty to hold her attention and she kept a sharp eye open for road signs—a map would have been handy...

'There's a map in the pocket beside you,' said the Professor. Was he a thought-reader or did he want to keep her occupied so that there was no need to talk? The latter, she decided, and opened the map.

South to Utrecht, on to Dordrecht and then Breda, where they stopped at a roadside café just outside the town. As they went in he said, 'Fifteen minutes. Coffee and a *Kaas broodje*?'

Julia had spied a door at the back of the cafe with Dames written above it in large letters, 'Anything,' she told him as she sped away.

The Professor got up and pulled out a chair for her when she returned to the table. The coffee was already there, so were the cheese rolls. Obviously this wasn't to be a social meal; they ate fast and silently and were away again with her mouth still full.

'Sorry to rush you,' said the Professor laconically.

To which she replied, 'Not at all, Professor.'

To tell the truth she was enjoying herself.

They bypassed Antwerp, took the road to Gent, bypassed Lille and flew on to Calais.

'Just nicely in time,' observed the Professor, going aboard the hovercraft with two minutes to spare.

He settled her at a small table by a window and said, 'Run along and do your hair; I'll order tea.'

It was early for tea, but the sight of the tea tray and a plate of scones gladdened her heart. The Professor, watching her pour second cups, thought how pretty she looked and how uncomplainingly she had sat beside him. The seat beside him might have been empty. Upon reflection he was glad that it hadn't been. A pity they couldn't like each other…!

They talked during the crossing, careful to talk about mundane things, and when he suggested that she might like to have a brief nap before they landed she closed her eyes at once, thinking that it was a polite way of ending their conversation. She wouldn't sleep, she told herself, but if she shut her eyes she wouldn't need to look at him…

A gentle tap on her shoulder woke her. 'Ten minutes before we land,' the professor told her. 'Run along before there's a queue.' He paused. 'And your hair's coming down.'

How was it, thought Julia, that her hair being untidy and going to the loo should seem so normal and unembarrassing between two people who didn't even like each other? She remembered with a shudder Oscar's coy references to powdering her nose, and the disapproving frown if she needed to stick a pin back into her hairdo.

There was no time to pursue the thought; they were

going through Dover and speeding along the motor-way to London without loss of time.

Saturday, she thought. She would have to race to the shops and get some food for the weekend. The idea of a cold house and an empty fridge didn't appeal, but of course a man wouldn't think of such things. No doubt, she reflected peevishly, the professor would go to wherever he lived when he had seen his patients and have a splendid meal set before him. She peeped at his calm profile; he appeared unhurried and relaxed but he certainly hadn't dallied on the way...

As they slowed through London's sprawling suburbs she began her rehearsed thank-you speech. 'It was very kind of you to give me a lift,' she began. 'I'm very grateful. I hope it hasn't held you up at all, me being with you. If you want to drop me off at a bus stop or the Underground...'

'You live very close to the hospital; it will be easier to take you to your house. Stopping anywhere here will hold me up.'

So much for trying to be helpful. She held her tongue until he stopped before her door. The house looked forlorn, as did the whole street, but she said brightly, 'How nice to be home—and so quickly.'

A remark which needed no comment as he got out of the car, took her case from the boot, the key from her hand, opened the door and ushered her into the narrow hall.

'Don't wait—' and that was a silly thing to say '—and thank you again.'

'A pleasure. Goodbye, Julia.'

He drove away without a backward glance.

'He's a detestable man,' said Julia fiercely, standing on her doorstep. 'I hope I never meet him again. Rushing me back home just because he was in a hurry. Well, I hope he's late for whatever it is.' She added rather wildly, 'I hope it's a beautiful woman who will make him grovel!'

He would never grovel, of course, and she didn't mean a word of it, but it made her feel better.

She went indoors then, and into the kitchen to be greeted by Muffin, and a moment later by Trudie, coming downstairs to meet her.

'I knew you'd be back. The man who brought the box said you'd be here some time today.'

Julia went to fill the kettle. 'Box? What box?'

'It's from some super shop in Jermyn Street. It's on the table.'

They went to look at it together. It was a superior kind of box, very neatly packed under its lid; tea and coffee, sugar, milk, a bottle of wine, croissants, eggs, cold chicken in a plastic box, a salad in another plastic box, orange juice, smoked salmon...

Julia unpacked it slowly. 'There must be a mistake.'

Trudie shook her head. 'I asked to make sure. The delivery man said there was no mistake. A Professor van der Maes had ordered it by telephone late yesterday evening to be delivered this afternoon.'

'Oh, my goodness. He never said a word. He gave me a lift back so that my sister's husband could stay in Holland for a day. We had to hurry to get to Calais and we only stopped once on the way. He had to get back by the late afternoon.'

'Well, it's a gorgeous hamper,' said Trudie cheerfully.

'It's coals of fire,' said Julia.

'Well, I'm going out this evening,' Trudie went on. 'You'll be all right?'

'Me? I'm fine, and thank you for keeping an eye on Muffin and the house. No one called about a room?'

'No. You had a good time?'

'It was heaven. I'll tell you some time.'

Presently, alone in the house, she unpacked, fed Muffin and got her supper. The contents of the box might be coals of fire, but they made splendid eating.

Presently, in bed, she lay awake composing a letter to the Professor. Fulsome thanks would annoy him, considering the coolness between them, all the same he would need to be thanked. She slept at last, only to wake from time to time muttering snatches of suitable phrases.

The letter, when it was at last written, was exactly right. Neatly phrased, politely grateful—and it would have served as a model letter for a Victorian maiden to have written. The Professor read it and roared with laughter.

The house, after the charming little cottage, was something Julia would have to get used to. Ruth, back home, had phoned her, bubbling over with the day she had spent with Tom and happy to be back in her little house. Julia had assured her that she was fine, that there was the prospect of a lodger and that the garden was looking very pretty. None of which was true. She didn't feel fine. For some reason she felt depressed.

And I'll soon deal with that, Julia told herself, and went off to the newsagent's to put a To Let sign in his window, and then back to mow the small square of grass in the garden.

There were two applicants for the room the next day. A foxy faced middle-aged man who smelled strongly of beer and wanted to cook his meals in the kitchen, and a youngish woman, skilfully made up, with an opulent bosom and very high heels, who said coyly that she was expecting to get married and would Julia have any objection to her boyfriend calling from time to time?

She told them that the room was already let and watched them go with regret. The rent money would have been useful...

Something would turn up, she told herself, and in the meantime she got a temporary job delivering the local directory. It was dull business, for the neighbouring streets all looked alike, as did the houses, but she enlivened the tedium of it by memories of the cottage, and at the end of the week there was a little money in her pocket and she had written in reply to six vaguely wanting help with houses and small children—something she could surely do without any kind of training. And it wouldn't be for long, she told herself. If could let a room—two rooms at a pinch—she could sleep in the box room.

She went to Ruth's for lunch on Sunday, and Thomas came over from the hospital for an hour or two. After the meal Ruth said, 'While you're here, Julia, would you look at that little chair I was going to cover? It's in the other bedroom and I've tried to do it, but it doesn't look right. You're so good at that kind of thing.'

So Julia went up the little stairs and into the second bedroom, which was small and unfurnished save for suitcases, a bookcase which was too large to go anywhere and the chair. It was a pretty little chair, and Ruth had pinned the velvet onto it in a haphazard fashion. Julia got down on the floor, undid it all to cut and fit, pinned and tacked, and sat back on her heels to study her work. It would do, but Ruth wanted a frill, she thought.

She was on the stairs when she heard Ruth's voice. The sitting room door was open and the house was small, with thin walls.

'Oh, Thomas, I can't ask Julia. Where would she go? But it would be wonderful. We'd have the money to start buying our own house, and Monica and George need central heating and a new bathroom— the house would sell for enough money for that?'

'Oh, yes, darling. Split three ways you would each get a very useful sum. But we mustn't think about it. If Julia marries you could suggest it then, but not before.'

Julia crept back into the room, closed the door quietly and sat down on the chair. Of course she had thought of it before, but had put it out of her mind. How could she have been so stupid? There was nothing remarkable about the house, but it had three bedrooms, and although the street was shabby it was quiet, and those who lived in it were law-abiding— striving to keep so. Moreover, there were buses and the Underground into the City. It would fetch a fair price—Ruth and Thomas could get a house of their own; Monica could have her central heating. As for herself...a small flat somewhere, and the money to take a course in something or other. She could think about that later. She would have to wait for a few days and then broach the subject...

Steps on the stairs sent her onto her knees, fussing with the frill.

Ruth put her head round the door. 'You had the door shut. You didn't hear me?'

'No. Were you calling? Look, do you want a frill? I think it would be too much.' She got to her feet. 'Has Thomas gone back? I'll come down, shall I?'

CHAPTER FOUR

THE opportunity to do something about the house came sooner than she had expected. Monica phoned to ask abut their stay in Holland, and when that subject had been exhausted she talked at length about George and the house and the village. 'I'm so happy, Julia…'

It seemed to be the right moment. Julia knew exactly what to say; she had rehearsed it carefully and now she made her suggestion with just the right amount of eagerness. 'I can't think why I haven't thought of it before. I haven't said anything to Ruth yet. Do you think it's a good idea? It's only an idea, anyway…'

She could hear the excitement in Monica's voice. 'But what about you?'

'I'd get a small flat and take a course in dressmaking. You know how I love making clothes.'

'Would we get enough from the house for all of us?'

'Yes, but perhaps Ruth wouldn't like the idea…'

'I'll talk to her and find out. Is this what you really want, Julia?'

'Oh, yes. Just think, I wouldn't have to depend on lodgers. I'd be free—have a holiday when I wanted to, come and go as I pleased and work at something I enjoy doing.'

She rang off presently, knowing that she had convinced Monica. Now she must wait and see what Ruth would decide, and let the news come from Monica.

She didn't have long to wait, Ruth phoned that evening. 'Monica rang and told me you'd suggested selling the house. But, Julia, what about you?'

So Julia repeated her carefully thought out words and added, 'Do you like the idea? It's only an idea...'

'You really want to? You'd be happier somewhere else? There would be enough money for you to feel secure?'

'I don't feel secure now,' said Julia. 'I need three lodgers to keep this house going and so far I've only got one; I didn't tell you that I got the sack from the greetings card people—but then I expected that; Oscar, you know. I could train as a dressmaker, live in a small flat...'

'Oh, my dear, I didn't know. I think it's a marvellous idea.' Ruth paused. 'As a matter of fact, Thomas and I have seen a house near the hospital—in a cul-de-sac, and so quiet. It's for sale...'

'You see,' said Julia bracingly. 'It's the hand of fate!'

Of course there was a good deal to discuss during the next few days. Julia, striking while the iron was hot, had the house valued, and the price the agent suggested clinched the matter. He had people on his books waiting for just such a house to come on the market. Ruth and Thomas, inspecting the house they so wanted to buy, had no doubts.

'A pity the Prof is away,' Thomas observed. 'By the time he gets back we'll probably have moved.'

'Will he be in Edinburgh much longer?'

'No, a few days more, but he's going straight to

Vienna to give lectures and then a week or two in Holland.'

'He'll have a nice surprise. Oh, Thomas, I do hope the house sells quickly.'

Something Monica hoped too, with her writing desk awash with central heating brochures and magnificent bathroom catalogues.

As for Julia, unaware that the Professor was away, she went to see the solicitor who held the deeds of the house, bullied the house agent in the nicest possible way, explained everything to Trudie and hoped that the hand of fate she had been so sure about would point a finger at her. Now that they were selling the house she wanted to be gone quickly, to start a new life. That she woke in the night to worry about that was something she did her best to ignore.

The house sold within a week. Moreover, it was a cash sale, and the new owner wanted to move in as soon as Julia could move out. Monica and Ruth came, and, helped by a cheerfully co-operative Trudie, they all set to work to pack up the house.

It wasn't just the packing up. There was the furniture—what was left after they had each decided what they wanted to keep and, since Trudie hoped to marry soon, she had had her share—and then the removal men, the gas, the electricity, the telephone, the milkman—an unending stream of things which needed her attention.

With three days left before the new owners took over Julia found herself in an almost empty house. Trudie had moved in with the other teacher at the kindergarten, George had driven up in a borrowed van and taken the furniture Monica had chosen, and the local odd-job man had collected the tables and chairs and beds which Ruth wanted for her new home. Which left Julia with a bed, a number of suitcases, a box of books, the kitchen table and two chairs. The fridge and cooker had been sold with the house, so meals were no problem although lack of comfort was. Ruth had wanted her to go and stay with them, but to leave the house empty was risky. And it was only for two nights.

Tomorrow, thought Julia, getting into bed with Muffin for company, she would go in search of a room to rent. She knew what she was going to do: find a small flat in a quiet street in a better neighbourhood. Islington would be nice, if she could find something to suit her purse. Perhaps a basement flat with a bit of garden at the back—or Finsbury—somewhere not too far from Ruth and Thomas. She wished that she had someone to advise her.

The Professor's face flashed before her closed eyes and she said out loud, 'What nonsense. He's not even in the country, and in any case he hasn't the least interest.'

Ruth had said that he was away, and that they hadn't told him that they were moving. 'We're going to surprise him,' said Ruth happily. 'He'll be back soon.'

'Not before I've gone,' reflected Julia now. 'Disagreeable man.'

She went in search of a room the next day and returned home disappointed. She had been to several likely addresses, but most of them had proved to be top-floor attics which wouldn't do at all for Muffin. One or two had been grubby, and the only one which would have done at a pinch she'd been denied. 'Not cats!' the lady of the house had said. 'Nasty, dirty creatures.'

'We'll try again tomorrow,' she told Muffin, inspecting the fridge for their suppers.

She was just finishing breakfast the next morning when there was a thump on the door. And when she went to open it there was the Professor.

She was aware of delight at seeing him, and that was something she would have to think about later on. For now she stared up at him wordlessly. His 'Good morning Julia,' was coolly friendly.

Since he stood there, obviously expecting to be asked in, she said, 'Oh, do come in—has something happened to Ruth or Thomas?' She shut the door behind him with something of a snap. 'It's very early…'

'This has nothing to do with Ruth or Thomas. I wished to talk to you.'

He stood in the hall, looking around him at the empty place. 'Is there somewhere…?'

She led the way to the kitchen, angry that he should see its poverty stricken appearance: the milk bottle on the table, a loaf of bread beside it, her mug and plate with a slice of bread and butter half eaten…

'Do sit down,' she begged him in a voice of a polite hostess who must entertain an unwelcome guest, and when he had taken the other chair at the table she asked, 'Would you like a cup of tea? There's still some in the pot.'

His mouth twitched. 'Yes, please,' he responded as his eye fell on the loaf.

'Would you like some bread and butter?' she asked.

'Breakfast is always such a pleasant meal,' he observed, before he cut a slice and buttered it.

'There's no need to be sarcastic,' said Julia. 'Why have you come?'

'It must be obvious to you that this is not a social visit. Unfortunately it is the only time of day when I'm free...'

She interrupted him. 'Ruth said you weren't in England.'

'I got back yesterday evening. Tell me, Julia, have you any plans for your immediate future?'

'Why do you want to know?'

'If you will answer my question I will tell you.'

'I can't see why you should ask, but since you have, no.'

'You have somewhere to go tomorrow? A flat or rooms?'

'No. I intend to find something this morning.' She frowned. 'I don't see that it's any of your business— and we're not even friends...' She blushed scarlet the moment she had said it and mumbled, 'Well, you know what I mean.'

'I hardly think that friendship has anything to do with it, and it is my business in so far that I am asking for your help.'

'Me? Help you?'

'If you would refrain from interrupting, I will explain.'

He drank his tea and looked at her. She was untidy, for she had done some last-minute packing; her hair was in a plait over one shoulder, she had a shiny nose, and was wearing a cotton top faded from many washings. But she looked quite beautiful, he thought. Her sisters were beautiful too, but Julia was full of life, impulsive, refusing to admit that life wasn't quite what she had hoped for. She had a sharp tongue, and a temper too...

He said gently, 'Indeed you could help me if you would consider it. You haven't forgotten Mrs Beckett? I have been with her for a day or two. She is ill—pneumonia—and in hospital. It is a viral infection and she isn't so young. Would you consider going over to Holland and minding the cottage while she is away, and then staying for a while when she gets back until she is quite well and I can arrange some sort of help for her?'

It was so unexpected that she could only gape at him.

'Go to Holland?' said Julia at length. 'But does Mrs Beckett want me—and how long would I be there?'

'Mrs Beckett will be very happy to see you again,' said the Professor smoothly. 'I cannot say for certain how long your stay might be. But she will be in hospital for at least two weeks, and when she returns home she will need a good deal of cosseting.'

'She is in hospital now?'

'Yes, in Leiden. A colleague of mine is the consultant physician there. I have arranged for someone to look after her cats and the cottage but it is a temporary arrangement. I want someone with no other commitments so that I can be sure that both Mrs Beckett and the cats and cottage are in the hands of a person who is willing to remain until she is quite fit.'

'But why me?'

He ignored that. 'I am aware that this may interfere

with whatever plans you have made. You would, of course, receive a salary and any expenses.'

'Well, I haven't any real plans. I mean none that can't be put off for a few weeks. There is no reason why I shouldn't go. When do you want me to be there?'

It was impossible to tell whether he was pleased or not. 'Within the next day or so. I will arrange for you to fly over. You will be met and taken to the cottage. You will be kept informed as to Mrs Beckett's condition and taken to visit her if you wish.'

He got up and she, perforce, got up too. His good-bye was brief and he had gone before the dozen questions tumbling around in her head could be uttered.

She had been glad to see him, she couldn't deny that, and not having to decide about her future for another few weeks was a relief she didn't admit to. It was while she was going through her scanty wardrobe that she started to wonder how he had known that she was leaving the house. Had he been back in England earlier and had Ruth told him? Surely he hadn't made up his mind to ask her in the space of a few hours?

It wasn't until she was getting her lunch that her eye fell upon Muffin…

The phone hadn't been transferred yet, thank heaven; moreover, she was put through to the Professor at once.

'Muffin,' she began without preamble. 'I can't go to Holland—Ruth's far too busy moving house and he'll pine in the cattery.'

'No problem. My housekeeper in London will be delighted to look after him. I have arranged for you to fly over tomorrow afternoon. I will come for you at midday and we can leave Muffin with her as we go.'

And he had hung up without giving her a chance to say anything.

She addressed Muffin. 'I've been a fool. I have allowed Professor van der Maes to make use of me. I must be losing my wits.' Although, she reflected presently, it would be delightful to stay in that cottage again, and it would give her time to decide exactly what she intended to do next.

She was ready for him when he came; the new owners were moving in later that afternoon, everything was signed and sealed, the money was in Ruth's care, and her share would be waiting for her when she got back. In the meantime she had enough of her own to keep her going. The Professor had mentioned a salary, but probably it had just been a passing thought.

He greeted her in a businesslike manner and stowed Muffin on the back seat, her case in the boot and herself beside him without more ado. She didn't look back as he drove away. She and her sisters had lived in the house but it had never been home to any of them.

She sat without speaking as he drove through the busy streets. Presently he said, 'I shall have to drive straight to Heathrow.'

He had shown no signs of impatience at the slow progress they were making, but a glance at the clock told her that at the rate they were going they would never get to the airport on time. All she said was, 'Muffin?'

'I will take the cat to my house as soon as I have seen you on to the plane. I promise you that I will see that he is in safe hands.' He gave her a quick look. 'Trust me, Julia.'

'Yes,' said Julia, knowing that she meant it.

She was the last to board the plane; there had barely been time to bid Muffin goodbye before she was hurried away, told that she would be met at Schipol and would she telephone him that evening?

'The phone number is in the envelope with your ticket. Goodbye, Julia.'

Schipol was overflowing with people; Julia stood for a moment, wishing wholeheartedly that she hadn't come, then a short, thickset man, bearing her name on a placard he was holding before him, came to a halt in front of her.

'Miss Gracey? Sent by Professor van der Maes? I am Piet, to drive you to his house.' His English was strongly accented but fluent.

Julia held out a hand. 'How do you do? Is it a long drive?'

'No, I drive fast.' He picked up her case and led the way through the crowds, out to the car, which was an elderly Mercedes. Its appearance, she quickly discovered, was deceptive; it was capable of a fine turn of speed which, coupled with Piet's obvious wish to be a racing driver, took them at a hair-raising speed to the cottage.

As she got out Piet told her that he would call for her in the morning and take her to see Mrs Beckett at Leiden. He took her case into the cottage, gave her a broad grin and was gone.

There was someone in the cottage, waiting for her:

a small woman with an old-fashioned hairdo, wearing a severe black dress. She smiled a welcome and broke into voluble speech, unfortunately in Dutch.

Julia smiled in return, offered a hand and mustered her few words of that language.

The woman was amused. 'I go. I come at morning, early.' She thought for a moment. 'Work, cook.'

'All day?'

'Mornings. Professor van der Maes tell.'

'I should hope so. How like a man,' said Julia crossly and her companion smiled and nodded. 'Nice man. Food ready. *Dag.*'

She trotted off in the direction of the village and Julia closed the door and found Mrs Beckett's cats staring at her.

'Well, at least I can talk to you,' said Julia, and at that moment the phone rang.

'You had a good journey?' enquired the professor. 'Mevrouw Steen was at the cottage?'

'Is that who she is? Why are you ringing me? You told me that I was to phone you this evening.'

'I thought that you might be anxious about Muffin. Why are you cross?'

'I am not cross.' She sounded peevish. 'I am in an empty house with two cats, I want a cup of tea, and *Mevrouw's* English is as basic as my Dutch.'

'An excellent opportunity for you to improve your knowledge of the language.'

'I have no wish to do so,' said Julia haughtily. 'Is there anything you wanted to say to me? Because if there isn't I'm going to put the kettle on...'

He took no notice. 'Piet will take you to see Mrs Beckett tomorrow morning. Arrange with her or the doctor when you wish to visit her and let him know. Piet will drive you wherever you should wish to go and do any odd jobs or errands for you

She said stiffly, 'Thank you. Is Muffin all right?'

'Settled down very nicely. I hope you will do the same, Julia.' With which he rang off.

'Rude man,' said Julia.

She had every intention of wallowing in self-pity as she went into the kitchen, but the sight of the tea tray standing ready on the kitchen table made her hesitate. There wasn't only a pretty teacup and saucer and plate on it, matching the teapot, sugar bowl and milk jug, but also a plate of buttered scones and a little dish of jam, and when she opened the fridge door while the kettle boiled she found salmon, ready to eat, and salad and a bowl of potato straws. Moreover, there were strawberries and cream and a bottle of white wine.

She made the tea, carried the tray through to the sitting room and wondered uneasily if she had been a bit too off-hand with the Professor...

Her bedroom welcomed her: flowers on the dressing table, a pile of books and magazines on the bedside table, a carafe of water and a tin of biscuits, and in the bathroom towels and soaps and a delicious selection of oils for the bath. Somebody had been very thoughtful about her well-being, she reflected, going downstairs and taking the bottle of wine from the fridge. She didn't feel lonely or hard-done-by any more; it was as though she had been warmly welcomed even if there had been no one there to do that.

Presently she ate her supper, drank the rest of her glass of wine, fed the cats and, accompanied by them both, went upstairs to lie in the bath and then get into bed. Her two companions settled each side of her and she hoped that Muffin was being as well cared for. She would be all right, she decided sleepily; the Professor had said that he would look after her...

She woke to a splendid morning; hanging out of the window, she looked down at the garden, which was a riot of colour, and beyond it to the flat, peaceful countryside... She showered and dressed and skipped downstairs, intent on breakfast. She had fed the cats and was eating her boiled egg when Mevrouw Steen arrived.

She greeted Julia with a cheerful *'Dag'* and then added, 'Piet comes; I stay.'

So Julia gobbled down the rest of her breakfast, found her handbag, got into Piet's car and was driven to Leiden—a trip she would have enjoyed if she hadn't been so scared of the speed at which Piet drove. But he was a splendid driver, and of course the road ahead of them was flat as far as the eye could see. He put her down at the hospital, rather shaken and glad to feel solid ground beneath her feet. He would return in an hour, he told her, and wait until she came. She was not to hurry.

Mrs Beckett, looking half her normal size, was propped up against her pillows with an oxygen mask clamped over her nose. But she smiled and nodded to Julia and waved a languid hand.

'Don't talk,' said Julia urgently. 'I'm going to sit here and tell you all the news!'

Mrs Beckett listened, nodding from time to time, then asked, 'Portly and Lofty—how are they?'

'Both in splendid health; they slept on my bed. You don't mind?'

Mrs Beckett smiled. 'I'm glad. Mr Gerard has been to see me. He'll come again; he's so good to me.'

'He's organised everything,' Julia assured her. 'As soon as you're well again you are coming home, and I'll stay until you are perfectly fit.'

'You'll want to go home,' whispered Mrs Beckett. 'To your own home.'

'I haven't got one. We've sold it. I'll find somewhere to live when I get back. It's lovely being here again. The cottage looks lovely and I'll look after everything.' She bent and kissed the pale cheek. 'I'm going now. I shall phone every day and come and see you again in a day or two. You are going to get well quickly; the Professor told me so.'

Which wasn't true, but a lie in a good cause...

'If he said so, then I shall.'

It was a relief but no surprise to find that the doctor she asked to see spoke English as good as hers. Mrs Beckett was making good progress, he assured her. She had been seriously ill—pneumonia in the elderly was not to be treated lightly—but she had responded well to treatment.

'You are a friend of Professor van der Maes?'

It would save a lot of explanations if she agreed...

'May I come at any time? Not every day, perhaps, but I will phone each morning and you will let me know at once if it's necessary.'

'Of course.'

He walked with her to the entrance, where Piet was waiting, and watched her getting into the car. A delightfully pretty girl, he reflected. Gerard had told him that she was a sensible young woman, very well able to look after herself and deal with any situation which might arise. And of course Gerard would come at once in an emergency....

After that first day Julia slipped into a gentle pattern of days. Visiting Mrs Beckett, even beginning to enjoy Piet's breakneck driving, cherishing Portly and Lofty, filling the cottage with flowers because she knew that Mrs Beckett would like that, weeding and tending the flowerbeds when the gardener allowed, practising her sparse Dutch on Mevrouw Steen and each evening listening eagerly for the phone to ring. The Professor never had much to say but his voice was reassuring.

She had been there for several days when he said, 'The question of your salary. I have arranged for my bank to send it to you each week in guilders.'

'I don't need any money,' said Julia.

'Money is something which everyone needs from time to time,' said the Professor, and hung up before she could utter another word.

When the postman brought it she sat at the kitchen table and counted it. There seemed to be a great deal, even when she did careful mental sums and changed it into pounds. 'For a month, I suppose,' she said and, feeling rich, went to the village and bought postcards, stamps and chocolate.

The following week the same amount arrived, so that evening when he phoned she pointed out to him that there had been a mistake; she already had her salary.

'Did I not make myself clear? Each week you will receive your money from my bank...'

'But it's too much.'

'I must beg you not to argue. When are you going to see Mrs Beckett?'

'Tomorrow, in the morning. Why?'

'If you will give me time to speak, I will tell you. She is so much better she will probably be able to come home within the next few days. She will need to convalesce in a leisurely fashion. I rely upon you to see that she does.'

'I'll take the greatest care of her. How will she come home? Shall I go with Piet and fetch her?'

'I will tell you in due course. In the meantime you will see her doctor tomorrow.'

'Very well.' Then she added, 'Don't you ever say goodbye?'

'Not to you, Julia.' And he hung up!

Mrs Beckett was sitting in a chair by her bed when Julia got to the hospital. She looked weary and far too pale, but Julia was pleased to see that she was taking an interest in life once more.

'I'm coming home soon,' she told Julia. 'I've missed it so…' Her eyes filled with tears.

'Won't it be fun? Lofty and Portly will be so glad to see you…the garden looks lovely, and so many people have asked me how you are. You have so many friends. They'll want to come and see you, but the doctor says you must be a bit quiet for a little longer.'

'I know. Mr Gerard told me. I'm to do what you say just for a time; he's promised that everything will be just as it always was.'

'Well, of course it will. And I promise you that I

won't make you do anything that you don't want to do.'

She hugged Mrs Beckett because she looked so small and frail.

'If the weather is warm and fine, you shall sit in the garden and tell me what to do.'

Four days later Julia was awakened by a thunderous knocking on the door.

'Mrs Beckett—something's happened,' she told the cats as she tore down the stairs, tugging on her dressing gown as she went, her feet bare.

The professor was on the doorstep.

'I didn't use my key; I didn't want to disturb you...'

'But you have disturbed me. You've given me the fright of my life—I thought something had happened to Mrs Beckett. And why are you here?'

'If I might come in?' he asked meekly. 'This is my home!'

He sounded meek, but he gave her a mocking smile as she stood aside to let him pass.

'Oh, well—sorry,' said Julia. 'You could have phoned.'

He agreed blandly; he hadn't known until the very last minute that he could snatch twenty-four hours away from his work; too late to warn her of his intention.

'Tea? Breakfast?' Julia went ahead of him into the kitchen and turned to look at him. It was then she saw how tired he was...

'You've had no sleep. How did you come? When do you have to go back?'

'Tonight. I've come to bring Mrs Beckett home.'

'You'll have a cup of tea, then go and sleep for an hour or so while I get breakfast. What time do you plan to go to Leiden?'

'Shortly after midday.'

She had the kettle on, was setting out mugs, sugar and milk. 'Mevrouw Steen won't be here before eight o'clock.' She got the loaf and butter and cut him a generous slice. 'What a good thing I made the beds up yesterday...'

He sat at the table, watching her. Her hair was all over the place, her dressing gown had come untied, her feet were bare. She was, he decided, just what a man would want to see after a sleepless and tiring night.

Julia, far too busy to bother about appearances, put his tea before him, cut him more bread and butter and poured herself a mug. 'There's plenty of hot water,' she told him. 'Did you bring the car?'

'Yes. I'll have a shower and a nap. Breakfast about nine o'clock?'

It was barely seven. 'Yes, would you like it in bed?'

He choked back a laugh. 'The last time I had breakfast in bed I was nine years old, suffering from the mumps.'

When she looked at him, he added, 'That was twenty-seven years ago.'

He smiled, and the smile made her suddenly aware of the flyaway dressing gown and no slippers. She said briskly, 'I will call you at nine o'clock.'

He went away then, and she saw to the cats, put everything ready for breakfast and went quietly upstairs. The bathroom door was open but the three bedroom doors were closed. She had a shower, dressed, then made her bed and went downstairs again. Just in time to say *dag* to Mevrouw Steen.

There was no need to tell her that the Professor was there; the car was before the door. Mevrouw Steen broke into voluble talk, smiling widely.

'Mrs Beckett is coming home today.' Julia thought for a moment and added in Dutch, 'This afternoon.'

Mevrouw Steen nodded. 'I clean house...'

She trotted off, but not before Julia had warned her not to go upstairs until the Professor was awake. 'No sleep,' she told her in her fractured Dutch. 'Driving all night.'

Mevrouw made sympathetic clucking noises, went into the sitting room and shut the door on the sound of the Hoover.

Julia began to get breakfast. Bacon and eggs, tomatoes, mushrooms, fried bread. There was no lack of food in the house. Toast and marmalade to follow, and tea or coffee. And while she was busy she considered lunch. Salad, and there was ham in the fridge, and in the evening before he went back she would cook him a meal. A Spanish omelette, potatoes in their jackets and a salad—a bread and butter pudding, perhaps, or a sponge pudding with custard...

The bacon was sizzling in the pan and it was nearly nine o'clock. Time to rouse him...

He came into the kitchen through the door leading to the garden.

'You're up,' said Julia, and frowned because that had been a silly thing to say.

'I wanted to have a quick look at the garden. Something smells delicious.'

He looked as though he had slept all night—shaved and immaculately turned out. Of course he would have clothes here, thought Julia, and, suddenly conscious that she had been staring at him, she blushed.

The Professor studied the blush with interest and decided that it made her even prettier than she already was.

'Can't I help?' He sounded casual.

'If you would make the toast?'

Mevrouw Steen came in then. She had a great deal to say and it was frustrating, for Julia only understood one word in a dozen. The dear soul paused for breath presently and Julia offered her a mug of coffee and she trotted off with it. She would go upstairs, she said, and clean.

'A good soul,' said the Professor as he speared a mushroom. 'When you leave here I must find some kind of help for Mrs Beckett. Mevrouw Steen's a splendid worker but she doesn't like responsibility.'

Julia looked down at her plate. 'I expect you would like me to go once Mrs Beckett is settled here.'

'Now, why should you think that? Mrs Beckett is going to need you for another three weeks at least. You wish to go home?'

'No, no. I love it here,' she burst out. 'I don't know how you can bear to live anywhere else. Well, I dare say that's not true, for you have your lovely house in Amsterdam.'

'You liked that too?'

'My goodness me, indeed I did.'

'Then we must find time to go there again.' He added casually, 'I am planning to do rather more work over here—go over to Scotland from time to time when necessary.'

'You mean you won't live in London?' The thought filled her with a dismay she couldn't understand.

The professor watched her face. 'From time to time,' he repeated gently. 'I'm going down to the village to see Piet. Shall we have lunch before we go to Leiden?'

'We? Wouldn't it be better if I stayed here and had everything ready—tea—and the cats waiting.' She looked at him. 'A welcome, if you see what I mean.'

He agreed readily, and presently she watched him walking along the lane. Even from the back he looked full of energy—a man who had had a good night's sleep and with not a care in the world.

CHAPTER FIVE

THE Professor didn't come back until she was putting lunch on the table. 'Well,' said Julia to Portly, sitting beside her while she made a salad, 'I'm sure if he doesn't want my company I couldn't care less. After all, I'm only a kind of housekeeper.'

She wallowed in a comforting self-pity for a few minutes, and then forgot about it as the Professor came into the kitchen.

'Piet will come each day,' he told her without preamble. 'He'll do anything you want him to do and if you wish to leave the place he will stay with Mrs Beckett and Mevrouw Steen.'

'Thank you, but I'm happy to stay here. Will Mrs Beckett be able to sit outside for a while each day?'

'Dr de Groot—you saw him at Leiden—will come and see her in a day or so and let you know what he wants done.'

'I see. When will you go back?'

'Anxious for me to be gone, Julia?' He sounded amused. 'I'm going back this evening.'

'But you've only just got here. You've had no sleep; you'll be dead on your feet.'

'I'm going back from Harwich on the night ferry. I'll sleep then.'

He drove away after lunch and she tidied up, put the tea things ready and went up to her room. She wasn't a vain girl, but she had the sudden urge to make the most of herself. It would have to be the same blue denim skirt, because she hadn't another, but there was a newly washed and ironed cotton blouse, and she wasted a good deal of time trying out various ways of doing her hair, only to tug out the pins and bundle it up on the top of her head. 'He won't notice anyway,' she told Lofty, watching her from the bed.

Of course he noticed, the moment he got out of the car and saw her waiting on the porch. He lifted Mrs Beckett out of the car and carried her into the cottage, and as he passed Julia he observed, 'I like the hair. Is it in my honour?'

She went pink, going ahead of him to open the sitting room door as he bore his housekeeper in and settled her in the chair Julia had put ready. Mrs Beckett said in a wispy voice, 'My dear, how well you look—such lovely pink cheeks. I do hope I'm not going to be too much of a nuisance.'

Julia gave her a gentle hug. 'What nonsense. I love being here and I shall love looking after you. I'm going to get the tea; you must be dying for a cup.'

She got herself out of the room and Mrs Beckett settled back in her chair and nodded her head. 'A dear girl, don't you agree, Mr Gerard?'

He grinned at her. 'Don't fish, Nanny. When we've had tea you're going to bed, and mind you do exactly what Julia tells you. I must give her all the details of your treatment before I go.'

Tea was quickly over, which was a good thing for Julia could think of very little to say. The Professor made gentle small talk, addressing her from time to time and staring at her in a way which both annoyed and disturbed her. His remark about her hair had shaken her calm—perhaps she should have taken more pains with it.

He'll be gone in a few hours, thought Julia, and for some reason her spirits sank.

Getting Mrs Beckett to bed took time. There were her things to unpack and put away and frequent pauses while she discussed the hospital and her illness. When Julia finally went downstairs she found the Professor in the kitchen.

'I must leave in just over an hour,' he told her. 'Come here and listen carefully to what I have to say.'

'You must have a meal before you go. You can still tell me while I'm cooking it.'

She had her nose in the fridge. 'A bacon omelette? Asparagus? New potatoes?'

'Excellent. If you are as handy with the frying pan as you are with the needle I am indeed a lucky man.'

'You have no reason to be sarcastic...'

'What do you intend to do when you get back to London, Julia?'

'Be a dressmaker. Only I must be taught properly first.'

'And where will you live?'

'Oh, somewhere...'

Since he didn't answer, and the silence got a bit lengthy, she added, 'Ruth and Thomas have found such a nice house; I expect you've seen it. And of course Monica and George have a lovely old vicarage...'

'And you, Julia—do you not wish for a home and a husband and children, or is the fashioning of garments the acme of your ambition?'

'I don't like you when you talk like this,' said Julia fiercely. 'Never mind me, and much you care anyway, just tell me what I must do to get Mrs Beckett on her feet again.'

He didn't speak for a moment, but looked at her with lifted eyebrows, and when he did speak he was Professor van der Maes, giving courteous instructions to a patient's attendant.

She listened carefully while she beat eggs and chopped bacon and mushrooms, and when he had finished said, 'Thank you, that's all quite clear, but please write her medicines down so that I can be quite sure.'

'And here is Dr de Groot's phone number. Don't hesitate to ring him if you feel the necessity.'

She set the potatoes to cook. 'Will you come again to see Mrs Beckett?'

'If it's possible. I have complete faith in de Groot. As for yourself, I think that Mrs Beckett will be fully recovered in three weeks. I shall arrange for suitable help before you return.' He wandered to the door. 'Will you let me know when my supper is ready? I'm going to sit with Nanny.'

It's my own silly fault, reflected Julia. Why can't we be friends? And why did he want me to come here if he dislikes me so much? Once I leave here I won't see him again; I'll find somewhere miles away.

Somewhere where—hopefully—she could make a living, find friends, perhaps meet a man who would want her for his wife. There must be any number of men around not in the least like Oscar, or, for that matter, the Professor. There was no one like him, she added...

She laid a place for him at the table, tossed the potatoes in butter and mint and had the pan hot ready for the omelette. She could hear the murmur of voices as she went into the hall when she called him and he came at once.

'There are strawberries and cream,' she told him, 'and I've made coffee.'

'Thank you. I've said goodbye to Nanny; she's a bit tearful, so I think a glass of claret might do her good before her supper. And you too, of course.'

He didn't talk much as he ate, and presently he went and got his bag.

She said awkwardly, 'I hope you have a safe journey and won't be too tired.' She had gone to the door with him. 'I promise I'll take good care of Mrs Beckett.'

He stood looking down at her. 'I'm sure of that. Look after yourself, Julia.'

He got into the car and drove away and she stood in the porch staring down the now empty lane. She felt empty too.

There were letters from Monica and Ruth in the morning; it was nice to know that selling the house had brought them so much happiness. And Monica wanted her to go and stay after she'd spent time at Ruth's, which solved the problem as to where she would go next. Somehow the future had seemed vague and far off, but the Professor had mentioned three weeks. In that time she must make up her mind what she intended to do.

Mrs Beckett was a model patient and, like a trusting child, did everything asked of her without question. Julia cooked her small tasty meals, helped her with the slow, tiring business of dressing and undressing, and after a few days led her carefully downstairs to sit and watch the TV or chat. Talking was something she enjoyed, and Julia was soon in possession of the professor's family history.

Old family, said Mrs Beckett, wealthy and respected. 'His father was a surgeon, you know. Retired now. His mother's a sweet lady. He has brothers and sisters too. A brother in Canada and two sisters in New Zealand. All married. His parents are visiting them and will be away for some months.'

'They live in Amsterdam?'

'No. No, dear. In den Haag. Mr Gerard took over the Amsterdam house when he came of age. Lovely old house too, but he needs a wife to run it...'

'I should have thought that the Professor would have had no difficulty in finding someone; he's rich and good-looking and well known in his profession.'

Mrs Beckett peered over her specs. 'Yes, dear, but Mr Gerard will never marry unless he finds his dream girl—he told me that a long time ago.' Before Julia could pursue the subject she added, 'I fancy a cup of tea. Make it in the brown pot, dear, it tastes so much better.'

It was in one of the numerous magazines Mrs Beckett had sent from England that Julia, idly leafing through its pages, saw the advertisement.

Skilful needlewomen were required to help in the repair of old fabrics and upholstery at a stately home in the north of England. Small salary and accommodation on the estate property. References would be required and full details as to the applicant's skill.

Interviews would be held in London in one month's time.

Just what I'm looking for, reflected Julia, and miles away from London. Although why that should be so vital a need was something she didn't enlarge upon, even to herself. That evening she sat down and wrote a letter...

The weather was delightful and Mrs Beckett, spending quiet hours in the garden with Lofty and Portly in close attendance, began to look like her former plump self. As for Julia, cooking tasty meals, washing and ironing, pottering around the garden, she found life was a pleasure which she would have liked to continue for ever.

Mevrouw Steen and Piet smoothed her path, and if they found her Dutch inadequate and frequently laughable, they were too kind to say so. She had little time to herself, though, for Mrs Beckett liked to have company and was sometimes fretful at having to sit quietly and watch activity which she would normally have enjoyed herself. But as the days passed and she began to take up her normal life again Julia gradually handed over to her. In another week she would be back to her normal state of health.

The thought of leaving depressed Julia, although she told herself that it was time she went back to England and got on with her own life. After all she had money now, and soon she could decide what she wanted to do...

A problem solved for her for one morning, when a letter arrived for her. If she cared to present herself at a certain London hotel on a day three weeks from now, she would be interviewed with the possibility of being employed at the stately home. She should bring with her two references and a sample of her needlework. She would be good enough to acknowledge the letter...

Which she did, without saying anything to Mrs Beckett, trusting to luck that she wold be free by then. That done, she expressed a wish to do some embroidery. 'So that I can sit with you and not feel guilty while you knit,' she explained, and wished that she could take Mrs Beckett into her confidence.

Mrs Beckett was enthusiastic: there was a box in the attic, full of bits and pieces. Julia could rummage around and take whatever she fancied.

She found the ideal thing: a piece of patterned damask and a bundle of silks. She set to work, embroidering the pattern in a variety of stitches and various colours, and Mrs Beckett, examining it, declared that it was a lovely piece of embroidery.

'What a clever girl you are,' she observed. 'It's almost professional.' And she smiled so fondly at Julia that she almost told her of her plans. But she couldn't, of course, otherwise Mrs Beckett might feel that she was anxious to be gone—which thought was followed by another: if she told her companion what she hoped to do, the Professor might come to hear of it, and it seemed of the utmost importance that he should be unaware of her plans for the future.

He came a few days later, coming unhurriedly into the garden where they were having tea. Mrs Beckett saw him first.

'Mr Gerard—what a sight for sore eyes. And just in time for tea!'

He bent to kiss her. 'You're well again, Nanny. You look splendid...'

He nodded to Julia, half smiling. 'Julia has done a splendid job.'

'I'll get a cup and saucer and more tea,' she said, and took herself off indoors. So she was to go, and quite soon. And was he staying? Because if he was she would have to make a room ready and reorganise supper. She put the kettle on and warmed a teapot, found a cup and saucer and plate and a tray to put them on, and picked up a knife to cut the cake on the table.

It was taken from her and the Professor cut an enormous slice and began to eat it.

'Are you hungry?'

'For a home made cake? Always—don't you know that the way to a man's heart is through his stomach?'

She spooned tea into the pot. 'Are you staying?' Her voice sounded wooden in her own ears. Why, oh, why did she feel so awkward with him?

'For supper. I flew over; Piet will drive me back to the airfield later. I wanted to see how Nanny was getting on. She's fit again, but I have asked Dr de Groot to come tomorrow and give her a check-up. If he agrees with me, I'll be over in a few days with a nice middle-aged woman who will take over from you. You will be glad to go home, Julia?'

He had eaten the cake so she cut him another slice. 'Oh, yes, although I've been happy here, but Mrs Beckett wants to get back to her normal life. This lady who is coming—does Mrs Beckett know her?'

'Yes. She used to work for my mother. They were

good friends and she will stay for as long as Nanny wants her to. I have told her and she's delighted.'

He picked up the tray and Julia followed him, the rest of the cake on a plate. She hoped that he would have time to tell her how Thomas and Ruth were and, more importantly, how she was to get back home. 'Home,' she muttered to herself. 'I haven't got a home…'

There was no talk of the return as they had tea, and it was Mrs Beckett who did most of the talking.

'I have never felt better,' she assured the Professor. 'This dear girl has looked after me as though she were my own daughter—all the delicious food she has cooked for me—I have grown quite plump. She chuckled. 'Julia says she has grown fat, but I tell her that she is just right—I like a woman to have a shape…'

Julia went pink and looked away, but not before the professor had caught her eye. 'You take the words out of my mouth, Nanny.'

Julia found his smile so disquieting that she jumped to her feet, declaring that she must see what there was for supper, and nipped smartly into the cottage. Safe in the kitchen, she shut the door, muttering to herself, and poked her head into the fridge, glad that she had something as prosaic as supper to take her mind off that smile.

She had made watercress soup earlier that day; there would be just enough for the three of them if she served it carefully. She had intended omelettes for the two of them, but now she took lamb chops from the fridge, scrubbed new potatoes, baby carrots and added to the broad beans. These on the Aga, she turned her attention to a pudding. Egg custards with plenty of cream...

That dealt with, she laid the table in the dining room. She and Mrs Beckett ate their meals in the kitchen, but for this evening Julia set the table as Mrs Beckett liked it, with flowers and a starched table-cloth, polished silver and the best glasses. It looked nice when she had finished it and it had been a good excuse to stay in the cottage. She went back to the kitchen, inspected the chops, and the Professor asked from the door. 'Can we talk now, or shall it be after supper?'

'Well, everything will be ready in ten minutes.'

'Ample time. You will want to know how you are to return home; it will take only a few minutes to tell you.'

So much for wanting the pleasure of her company, thought Julia, and clashed the saucepan lids with unnecessary noise.

She said, 'Well?' in an icy voice, and didn't look at him.

'If everything is as I hope it will be, I will come on Saturday—that's three days away. I shall bring with me Miss Thrisp, who has been here before and is already in possession of the facts of Nanny's illness. I want to leave after lunch. I shall have the car and we will go back by ferry.'

'Very well.' She added, 'Thank you.'

'Where will you go?'

'I'm staying with Ruth and Thomas for a while, and then Monica's asked me.'

'And after that?'

When she didn't answer he said carelessly, 'Oh,

that isn't any of my business, is it? If supper's ready I'll pour us some sherry. When does Nanny have her glass of red wine?'

'With supper. Piet brought a case of claret; we've had some of that.'

'Good. I'll fetch Nanny in and bring you your sherry.'

Julia gave the potatoes a prod. 'Thank you.'

He came back presently with the sherry and put it on the table. 'You're as cross as two sticks,' he observed cheerfully. 'Was it because I admired your shape?'

Julia, her back to him, tossed back the sherry. 'Certainly not. I hope I'm not so childish...'

'Not childish, Julia, but very much a woman. Give me those dishes; I'll carry them to the table.'

It must be the sherry, decided Julia, making her feel peculiar. And she had every intention of forgetting what the Professor had said, or rather the manner in which he had said it. Had he been poking fun at her? Trying to annoy her? She found that hard to believe; he wasn't that kind of a man.

He left soon after their meal, thanking her pleasantly for his supper. He might annoy her but she had to admit that he had lovely manners. When he had gone she cleared away and settled Mrs Beckett in her chair, then sat and listened to that lady's reminiscences of the van der Maes family and the Professor in particular. 'Always knew what he wanted to do, yet he found the time to backpack round the world, spent his holidays working for them poor starving children in Africa, and a year or so ago he went with a team to Bosnia. Not a word to anyone, mind you.'

Mrs Beckett settled herself more comfortably in her chair. 'You'd never think it to look at him, would you? And he don't lack for social life, either. Could have married half a dozen times, and when I remind him—respectful, of course—that it is time he settled down with a wife and had children, all he says is he hasn't found his dream girl. Although goodness knows it wasn't lack of trying on the part of various young ladies.'

She peered at Julia over her specs. 'I dare say you've wondered about him, Julia?'

A truthful girl, Julia pondered her reply. 'Well, a bit, sometimes. But you see, Mrs Beckett, we don't know each other very well. Circumstances brought us together, but once I've left here I dare say I shan't see him again. You see, I have nothing to do with hospitals, and I don't know anyone he might know.'

'Such a pretty girl. I can't believe that you haven't had a boyfriend.'

'Well, hardly that…' She told her about Oscar then, and Mrs Beckett nodded her head when Julia explained why she had run away from the hotel. 'Quite right too, nasty man. How fortunate that Mr Gerard happened to be there.'

'Yes, he was very kind and helpful. Now, I'm going to get your hot milk and see you to your bed; it's been a busy day.'

'Yes, but a most interesting one,' said Mrs Beckett thoughtfully.

Lying cosily in her bed presently, Mrs Beckett reflected that the pair of them were ideally suited. It was to be hoped that they would discover that for themselves as soon as possible, though it seemed likely that Mr Gerard had already done that...

Ruth phoned in the morning. It would be lovely to have Julia to stay, and she was to make herself at home for as long as she wanted to. Thomas was busy at the hospital, but they could go shopping and there was such a lot of talking to do. 'And then Monica wants you to go and stay with them, so don't hurry to get yourself settled. I'm not sure when you'll arrive exactly, but I'll be home waiting for you.'

Julia should have felt happy and content that her future was arranging itself so pleasantly. First Ruth, then Monica, and then, if she was lucky, the job at the stately home.

'I'm free as air,' said Julia, and wished that she weren't.

Three days had never gone so fast. Julia and Mevrouw Steen got a room ready for Miss Thrisp, and while Mevrouw Steen polished and Hoovered Julia did the flowers, stocked the fridge with the food Piet went to buy for her and then did her own packing. That didn't take long, for she had had no chance to buy anything other than small necessities from the village. She would buy clothes when she got home; the money she had been sent each week was almost untouched. She allowed her mind to dwell on the pleasant prospect of buying the kind of clothes she hankered after. No more curtains, she promised herself. She would gather together an elegant wardrobe. It was a pity that the Professor would never see her in it...

There had been no word from him, but she hadn't expected it. Dr de Groot had seen Mrs Beckett, pronounced himself satisfied, observed that Julia had taken good care of his patient and gone again. Presumably the Professor didn't think it necessary to add to that.

She was up early, anxious to have everything just so before he and Miss Thrisp came; she organised fresh flowers, salad and cold meat in the fridge, strawberries and cream, plus a selection of cheeses; Miss Thrisp might not want to spend time in the kitchen after her journey. Julia had coffee ready too, and some of the little almond biscuits Mrs Beckett had shown her how to bake. As for that lady, Julia had made sure that she looked her best, sitting now in the sitting room, a good breakfast inside her, her hair just so...

Julia went to do her own hair then. There was too much of it, she thought impatiently, tugging it viciously. Perhaps she would have it cut really short. It was the fashion, and it would be nice to be fashionable.

The Rolls stopped without a whisper of sound and the professor got out and opened the car door for Miss Thrisp. Julia, who had conjured up several mental pictures of her, was pleased to see that she was exactly as anyone with a name like that would look, being tall, and thin, with a long face and a long thin nose, very dark eyes and a mouth which would stand no nonsense. But her smile was warm and friendly, and Julia thought that, despite the nose, she was rather nice. Well, she would be, she reflected, ushering the pair of them into the cottage, otherwise the Professor wouldn't have allowed her near Nanny.

And why should I be so sure of that? she wondered. She left them in the sitting room after their brief introduction and a casual nod from the Professor, and went to the kitchen to fetch the coffee. She dawdled over that to give them time to exchange their first greetings, and presently, when she took the tray in, she found the two ladies sitting side by side, both happily talking their heads off. The Professor had gone to the open window and was looking at his garden.

He turned to face her as she put the tray down.

'We shall leave directly after lunch,' he told her. 'You're ready?'

She wondered what he would say if she said that no, she wasn't; he so clearly expected her to be waiting, case in hand.

She said, 'Yes. At what time do you want lunch?'

'Noon. So that there is ample time for goodbyes.'

She said tartly, 'Will you come and sit down for your coffee?' Once everyone had coffee and biscuits, she sat down herself and joined in the ladies' conversation.

Miss Thrisp was shown to her room, then went to the kitchen with Julia to make sure she knew where everything was. Before she went back to the sitting room she put a bony hand on Julia's arm. 'You've taken such good care of Mrs Beckett; I couldn't have done better myself. I'd have come the moment the Professor told me she was needing someone, but I was getting over a nasty attack of flu myself and I was real bothered as to what would happen. But he was right, you're worth your weight in gold—he never makes mistakes about people. You look exactly as he described you.'

It would have been nice to have known just what that was, thought Julia.

Lunch was a cheerful meal, but they didn't linger over it. Julia helped Miss Thrisp clear the table and then, obedient to the Professor's look, fetched her case and made her goodbyes.

Mrs Beckett was inclined to be tearful. 'But of course you'll come again?' she asked hopefully, and Julia mumbled that perhaps she would, if and when she had got settled.

'You must get Mr Gerard to bring you over for a weekend.'

Julia mumbled again, shook Miss Thrisp's bony hand, and got into the car, to turn and wave to the two ladies and the cats as they drove away.

The Professor had had little to say, but he had been pleasant in a remote kind of way and there were several things that she wanted to know.

'Where does the ferry leave from and at what time?'

'The catamaran—it leaves tomorrow around two o'clock, and gets to Harwich in the early evening.'

'Tomorrow? You mean today?'

'I mean tomorrow. We are spending the night in Amsterdam.'

She sat up very straight. 'You may be Professor, but I'm going back today.'

'Why are you making a fuss? A few hours more or less can't make a difference to your plans, but it is a matter of urgency that I stay until tomorrow.'

'I should have been told; I could have made other arrangements. I have no wish to stay in Amsterdam. And where am I to go, pray?'

'To my house, of course. Where else? And don't worry; I shan't be there. Wim and my housekeeper will take care of you.'

'Why won't you be there?' she asked sharply.

'I shall be at the hospital, operating early this evening, and I shall be there all night until I judge my patient to be in a stable condition. I hope that satisfies you?'

She felt mean. 'I'm sorry I snapped, but if you'd told me that when I first asked I wouldn't have said anything more about it.'

He didn't answer, and she added cautiously, 'Won't you be too tired to travel tomorrow?'

His 'no' discouraged her from saying another word.

But presently she asked, 'Why do we quarrel?'

'I never quarrel, and nor, I think, do you. We strike sparks off each other, Julia.' He turned his head briefly and smiled at her, 'And that's as good a beginning as any.'

She was about to ask him what he meant, but then thought better of it, and they stayed silent as they neared Amsterdam, but it was a friendly silence.

The quiet street by the canal seemed remote from the bustling streets of the city, the old houses silent under the trees which bordered it.

It's like coming home, reflected Julia as Wim opened the door to them and greeted her as though he had known her all his life.

The Professor spoke to him quietly and he nodded and went away, to return with a solidly built elderly woman who listened to what the Professor had to say, smiled at Julia and beckoned her to follow.

'This is Getske, my housekeeper,' the professor

said. 'Go with her; she will show you to your room. We have time for tea before I have to go.'

Julia followed the housekeeper along the hall and up the staircase at its end. It opened onto a circular gallery with passages leading off it and any number of doors. Getske opened a door and stood aside for her to go into the room beyond. It wasn't a large room but was instantly welcoming, with its canopied bed, the dressing table to one side, a small upholstered chair with a table beside it under the long window and a soft carpet underfoot. Through a door in the far wall there was a bathroom, and leading from it a wardrobe fit to house more clothes than Julia would ever buy.

Alone, she prowled round, picking things up and putting them down again. Then, remembering that the Professor might want to leave, she tidied her person, stuck a few more pins in her hair, dabbed powder on her nose and went back downstairs.

He was waiting with well-concealed impatience in a little room leading from the hall. Really, the house was a rabbit warren, she thought, but a very luxurious one and very much to her taste.

Tea had been laid out on a small table between two chairs. The Professor got up from one as she went in and Jason pranced to meet her.

'He will keep you company this evening.' The professor drew up a chair for her. 'Will you be Mother?'

She sat down and picked up the silver teapot. She would miss this elegance, she reflected. It was something she had become accustomed to during the last few weeks. The thought saddened her.

The Professor had his tea, ate a slice of cake and got up to go.

'I'll see you tomorrow morning,' he told her. 'Wim will take you round the house if you would like that—ask for anything you want.'

He was standing in front of her, looking down at her upturned face.

'Oh, I should like that; it's a lovely old house.' She smiled at him, and he bent down and kissed her. It was a gentle kiss, so why did it arouse such strong feelings in her person? She wondered, watching the door close behind his vast back.

Wim's English was as sparse as her Dutch, but they contrived to understand each other well enough. He had been with the Professor's family, he told her, for fifty years or more, and they and the house were his life. With Jason at their heels, they went from room to room, taking their time, while he pointed out the plasterwork ceilings, the heavy brocade curtains at the tall windows, the bow-fronted display cabinets filled with porcelain and silver, the exquisite marquetry on a long-case clock. Julia looked at it all with delight, wishing that the Professor was there too, so that she could tell him what a splendid home he had.

The house was surprisingly large, with rooms opening from one to another until the final one opened onto a long narrow garden. Tomorrow, she promised herself, she would explore the garden early in the morning, before the professor got home.

Wim took her upstairs then, waiting patiently while she poked her nose round each door on each landing, until they reached the final narrow staircase to the attic. When Wim smiled and nodded she took a look, then climbed up to the small door and opened it. The attic was long and narrow, with small windows at each end and a steeply sloping roof. It wasn't empty, containing odds and ends of furniture, rolled up rugs, a row of ice skates hanging from hooks on the wall and a baby's cradle. In one corner there was a stack of framed pictures and old photographs. She bent to look and picked up the top one. A boy, a quite small boy. She didn't need to read the date and name on it. She put it down again, feeling as though she had pried into the Professor's private life. He was smiling in the photo and his smile hadn't changed...

She had dinner in the same small room where they had had tea: watercress soup, duckling in an orange sauce and *pofferjes* light as air and smothered with cream. There was a light white wine, and coffee to follow, and a beaming Wim to serve her.

It was a reward for looking after Mrs Beckett, she supposed; he had paid her wages, but he could hardly tip her...

She offered a morsel of the little sugary biscuit which had come with the coffee to Jason and allowed herself to daydream. But presently she sat up. She had allowed her thoughts to run away with her just because the professor had kissed her.

'I shall go to bed,' she told Jason, and did so.

She was awake after a dreamless sleep when a stolid young girl brought her tea. She showered and dressed and went down to the hall and found Wim. Breakfast would be in half an hour he told her; the Professor wasn't home.

So she went into the garden and walked with Jason up and down its narrow paths in the morning sun. It was full of old-fashioned flowers, with a circular rose bed and flowering shrubs against the brick wall at its end. She could have stayed there, sitting on the rustic seat, surrounded by honeysuckle and wisteria, but breakfast waited.

The Professor was standing by the window of the room leading to the garden. His good morning was pleasantly friendly, his enquiry as to whether she had had a good night uttered in the tones of a thoughtful host. He was immaculately dressed and one would have supposed that he had enjoyed a good night's sleep too, but Julia saw the tired lines in his face.

'Have you had any sleep?'

'Enough,' he told her, and smiled so that she remembered the little boy in the photo.

I must forget that, she told herself, and went with him to eat her breakfast. They ate in silence for a time until she asked, 'Was it successful? The operation? Or would you rather not talk about it?'

He didn't answer at once, and she said quickly, 'All right, you don't have to tell me. I'm not being curious, you know.'

He loaded butter onto toast. 'It was entirely successful. And I don't mind you asking, Julia.' He stared at her across the table. 'I think that I would have been disappointed if you had not done so.' He passed his coffee cup. 'A mutual interest is to be desired.'

'Oh, is it?' said Julia, bewildered. She had a feeling that things were moving too fast for her to understand, but she was aware of a pleasant excitement. And they had the rest of the day together.

CHAPTER SIX

JULIA'S pleasant speculations about the morning were quickly cut short.

'We shall need to leave here after an early lunch,' said the Professor. 'I shall go back to the hospital presently, and I'll take Jason with me and give him a run. Perhaps you want to explore or go to the shops? I would be easier in my mind if you stayed here…'

She said brightly, 'I shall sit in the garden. I can do all the shopping I want when I get home.'

So he went away with Jason and she went into the garden again and sat down with the newspapers Wim had handed to her. She could so easily have gone with him, she thought; perhaps waited in the car while he was at the hospital, and then gone with him and Jason. He was deliberately avoiding her…

'I couldn't care less!' said Julia, and picked up the *Daily Telegraph* and read it from front to back page. She was none the wiser when she had. She tried the *Haagsche Post* next—she might as well improve her Dutch while she could—although it was a complete waste of time. She was puzzling out the small ads when the Professor joined her.

He said affably, 'Oh, splendid, you're improving your Dutch.'

'I have very little Dutch to improve,' said Julia coldly. 'I hope your patient is improving.'

112

He sat down beside her with Jason squeezed between them.

'Yes, I think he has a very good chance. I've left him in good hands.'

'Was he someone important?' She turned to look at him. 'Did they send for you specially?'

'Yes, and yes. Will you be sorry to leave Holland?'

'Oh, yes, although I've not seen anything of it. I'm sorry to leave the cottage and this splendid house, but they'll be lovely memories.'

'You would like to come back some time?'

'Perhaps.' She put an arm round Jason's woolly shoulders and he licked her hand gently. 'Jason is going to miss you.'

'Yes, and I shall miss him, but I shall be here again very shortly and he is used to my coming and going.'

He glanced at his watch. 'We had better have our lunch.'

The day which had seemed to stretch before her for hours of delight had telescoped into an all too short day. The professor might not like her, but that couldn't prevent her from enjoying his company. She supposed that she didn't like him either, but she was no longer quite sure about that. Of course, there was still the journey back to London...

Which was disappointing, in so far that the Professor, while thoughtful for her well-being, made only the most casual conversation, giving her no opportunity to get to know him better. On board, he excused himself smiling and began to study a case full of papers—first, however, making sure that she had something to read and a tray of tea.

She leafed through the magazines and wondered what he was thinking about.

She would have been astonished to know it was herself. Usually so sure of himself, the Professor found himself uncertain. That he had fallen in love with Julia and wanted her for his wife he now freely admitted, but she had shown no preference for his company; he thought that she liked him a good deal more than she was prepared to admit, but he wasn't prepared to rush her. Once back in London, he would have the opportunity to see her frequently. In the meantime, it was only by maintaining a casual disinterested manner that he was able to keep his hands off her...

They discussed the weather, the countryside and the state of the roads as he drove back to London. All safe subjects which lasted them nicely until he drew up before Thomas's and Ruth's new home.

They were warmly welcomed but the Professor didn't stay. He had a brief smiling chat with Ruth, observed that he would see Thomas at the hospital in the morning, and got back into the Rolls, brushing aside Julia's careful little speech of thanks.

He couldn't have been pleasanter, she thought, or more remote.

Mrs Potts, his housekeeper, and the two dogs were waiting for him. His housekeeper was middle-aged, brisk and devoted to him, and as for Wilf and Robbie, their welcome was estatic.

He took the car round to the mews at the back of

the house, promised to be back for his dinner and took the little dogs for a run. The streets were quiet; London on a summer's evening could be delightful. He thought about the cottage—he would have to ring Nanny when he got back—and he wondered if Julia was thinking of it too. She had loved the house in Amsterdam; she would fit so easily into his life...

Despite his casual goodbye, Julia had expected to see him again while she was staying with Ruth, but, beyond saying that he was working too hard, Thomas had nothing to say about him. Ruth wondered from time to time why he hadn't come to see them or at least phoned, but Julia's monosyllabic replies led her to a rather thoughtful silence. Julia looked splendid: full of fresh air, nicely tanned, apparently well pleased with life—and yet there was something wrong...

Ruth entered into the plans Julia had for an entire new wardrobe, and when she wasn't there phoned Monica. 'She looks marvellous, but there is something wrong. Do you suppose she met someone in Holland? She's coming to stay with you—try and find out.'

Getting ready for bed, Ruth asked Thomas, 'Has Gerard said anything about Julia?'

'Only that she has been a splendid help with Mrs Beckett. He's off to Glasgow tomorrow. He'll be gone for a couple of days.' Thomas gave her a sharp look. 'Why did you ask?'

'Oh, nothing, darling. They don't get on, do they?'

Thomas got into bed. 'Don't they? It isn't something I'd ask him—or Julia, for that matter.'

There were still ten days before her interview for the job. Beyond telling Ruth vaguely that she had heard of something, Julia had said nothing; instead she and Ruth went shopping.

With money in her purse Julia ignored the High Street chain stores and poked around boutiques, and, egged on by her sister, spent a good deal more than she had intended to. But the results were worth it; she bought well-cut jersey dresses, elegant tops and skirts, dresses for summer and a silk dress suitable for the evening. She thought that she might never wear it, that it would probably hang in the cupboard forgotten and regretted, but there was always the chance that she might need it—supposing the Professor should ask her to dine with him one evening?

It was highly unlikely—and even if he asked her she might refuse...

There were undies to buy too, shoes, a raincoat, a short jacket, a sensible outfit to wear if she got that job...

Afterwards she went to stay with Monica and George. She had a long weekend in which to explore their home and the village and listen to George preaching a splendid sermon. He had a good congregation too, said Monica proudly and she herself ran the Mothers' Union and Sunday School. Village life suited her, and now there was money to see to the plumbing and refurbish the vicarage. There was so much to see and talk about that no one noticed that Julia had almost nothing to say about her stay in Holland once she had given a brief account of it— and an even briefer reference to the professor.

Back with Ruth, she dressed in one of the jersey

dresses and, for once very neat about the head, went to her appointment. It was to be held in one of the smaller hotels and, urged by the porter to take the first door on the left of the foyer, Julia did so. There were five or six other women there, all armed as she was with specimens of their handiwork. They paused in their talk to stare at her, answer her good morning with nods and then resume their chatting. There was one older woman who had smiled at her, but others were young, smartly dressed and discreetly made up. Julia decided that she had very little chance against their self-assurance. Probably they had all been to a needlework school and had diplomas and marvellous references.

They were called in, one after the other, and came out looking pleased with themselves. The older woman went in, looking anxious, and when she came out she said nothing, only smiled again as Julia opened the door in her turn.

There were three women sitting behind a table. They greeted her pleasantly, told her to sit down, and the one in the middle, middle-aged and looking how one would imagine a strict schoolteacher would look, asked her why she wanted the job.

This was unexpected; there was no time to prepare a speech. Julia said, 'I want to get away from London,' and then wished that she hadn't said it, so she added, 'And I like needlework and sewing and making things out of things.'

The three women looked at each other. 'Will you show us your work?'

So she unwrapped the tapestry, its pattern picked out with the silks Mrs Beckett had given her, and spread it out on the table and sat down again. It was passed from one hand to the other, looked at through magnifying glasses and held up to the light. She was asked which stitches she had used and why she had chosen to embroider the tapestry.

'I hadn't anything else. I was in the country with no shops for miles. So I used what I found in the attic.'

'You understand that this is temporary employment? A week's notice on either side. Tedious work, repairing very old curtains. Quite long hours and the remuneration is small. Bed and board is free, of course. We are prepared to employ you on those terms.'

Julia didn't give herself time to think. She said, 'Thank you; I should like the job.'

'It will be confirmed by letter and you will be given directions as to how to reach the estate. You will need to go to Carlisle and then to Haltwhistle, where you will be met. Are you free to travel within the next day or so?'

'Yes, I can be ready in two days' time.'

Back in the waiting room, she found the older woman still there.

She said hesitantly, 'I waited. I thought they might take you. I've got a job there.'

'You have? I'm glad—so have I. Perhaps we could travel up together. Do you know that part of the world?'

'I was born near the estate. I came to London with my husband. He died and I wanted to go back home.'

'I'm sorry about your husband. I just wanted to get away from London.'

They were standing on the pavement outside the hotel 'Do you have a phone number? Perhaps we could meet at the station?'

The woman nodded. 'My name's Woodstock— Jenny. It would be nice to travel together.'

It wasn't difficult to convince Ruth that the job was something which was exactly what she had hoped for. 'And,' she pointed out, 'it isn't a permanent one; I expect that once the repairs are made we shan't be needed. And while I'm there I can decide where I want to live and what I want to do.'

Ruth said, 'Yes, dear,' in an uncertain way. Something was wrong. Perhaps Julia *had* met someone in Holland? She was about to ask when Julia said casually, 'Ruth, don't let the Professor know where I am. Don't look like that. It's just that he has this way of turning up with some offer of a job or something…'

It sounded pretty feeble but Ruth, thinking her own thoughts, said at once, 'I won't say a word. It sounds rather fun, this job. It's a long way away, of course, but probably it will be a lovely old house full of treasures and you'll meet lots of people.'

The day before she was due to leave the Professor came. Ruth had gone to the hairdresser and Julia was in the kitchen getting lunch when he knocked on the door. She had opened it expecting the postman, and the sight of the Professor standing there, smiling a little, did things to her breath. She had wanted to see him just once more, for after she had gone from London she had every intention of forgetting him. On the other hand she would have liked to have gone away before he found out that she was no longer at Ruth's.

She said now, 'Oh, hello. Did you want Ruth? She's out...'

'I came to see you.'

There was nothing for it but to ask him in. 'I'm getting lunch,' she told him, and led the way to the kitchen. It would be easier to calm down if she had something to do. And why should she need to calm down? she wondered.

'You're glad to be back?' he asked.

She whisked eggs in a bowl and didn't look at him. 'Yes, yes, I am.'

'Will you have dinner with me tomorrow evening, Julia?'

It was so unexpected that she put the bowl of eggs down with something of a thump on the table. 'Tomorrow? No—no, thank you.'

She looked at him then, wishing with her whole heart that she wasn't going miles away, knowing suddenly that she loved him and that the thought of not seeing him again was unbearable.

She said carefully, 'I'm sorry, I can't...I wasn't going to tell you—I'm going away—tomorrow morning.'

Something in his quiet face made her add, 'I've got a most interesting job. I want to get away from London...'

'You were not going to tell me?' His voice was as quiet as his face.

'No—no, I wasn't.' She had spoken too loudly, and now added recklessly, 'Why should I?'

'Indeed, why should you?' He smiled gently. 'I hope that you will be very happy.'

'Of course I shall be happy,' said Julia in a cross voice, wishing that he would go so that she might burst into tears in peace.

Which was exactly what he did do, blandly wishing her goodbye, telling her cheerfully that he would see himself out.

She wept into the eggs then, and, since she couldn't see to do anything for a moment, sat down and buried her face in Muffin's furry body. Muffin, who loved her in his own cat fashion, bore with the damp fur and Julia's incoherent mutterings, but it was a relief when she settled him back in his chair. Feline instinct warned him that she was unhappy, that she was probably going away. But she would be back, and in the meantime he was quite comfortable with Ruth. He settled down for a nap and Julia went and washed her face, and then went back to the eggs.

Ruth, back home again, took a quick look at Julia. 'You don't have to go, dear. You know you can stay here as long as you like, and if you want to get away from London, Monica would love to have you.'

She went to the fridge and poured two glasses of white wine. 'Is that a soufflé? It looks delicious...'

Presently Julia said, 'The Professor came. I told him I was going away but he doesn't know where I'm going. Don't tell him, Ruth.'

'Of course not, love.' Ruth was brisk. 'Did he want to know?'

'No,' said Julia bleakly. She added, 'He didn't even say goodbye.'

Ruth forebore from pointing out that he was a man

who never said anything he didn't mean. She began
to talk instead about the morrow's journey.

Jenny Woodstock was at the station in the morning,
mildly excited and happy at the thought of going back
to her home. She talked in her quiet way about it
during their journey and Julia was thankful for that,
for it kept her own thoughts at bay. And she was glad
to have someone with her who knew her way about
once they reached Carlisle and, finally, Haltwhistle.

Even then their journey wasn't over. There was a
middle-aged man, stocky, with a Land Rover waiting
for them, and they drove for what seemed like hours
through the wide countryside until he turned into a
wide gateway and onto a long drive. They could see
their destination now, an imposing mansion with a
few trees around it. Even on a summer's day it looked
bleak, but as they neared it Julia could see that it was
lived in and that there were cars parked to one side
of the house and people going in and out of the great
entrance.

Mrs Woodstock enlightened her. 'They're open to
the public twice a week.'

And the driver said over his shoulder, 'I'll drive
you round to one of the side doors. The housekeeper
will settle you in.'

A surly man, thought Julia. She hoped that the
housekeeper would be more friendly.

Her hopes were realised. Mrs Bates was large and
stout, with twinkling eyes and a wide smile. She offered tea and then led them out of the house and
across a wide courtyard. 'Most of the sewing ladies
come from the village,' she explained. 'I've put you

here, Mrs Woodstock.' She opened a door in one of the outbuildings. 'It's a nice little room and there's a bathroom and a gas ring and so on, so's you can be cosy.' She looked at Julia. 'If you'll wait here, Miss...'

She was back in a few minutes. 'You're over here, up these steps.' She observed, 'The place is used for storage but you won't be disturbed.'

She surged up the steps and unlocked the door at the top, and Julia followed her. The room was quite large, with a low ceiling and a wide window. It was comfortably furnished—a divan bed, a table and two chairs, an easy chair and bookshelves. There was another door leading to a shower room and an alcove with a gas ring and cupboards.

'You'll eat over in the house but I'll see you have tea and milk so that you can have a drink in your own room. You'll be wanted in half an hour or so. Will you come back to me and I'll take you?'

Left alone, Julia took another look around her; it was nice to have a room of her own, away from the house, and once she had unpacked and put her small possessions round the place it would look more like home. She tidied herself and then went in search of Jenny.

Jenny was delighted. 'It's like a hotel,' she observed happily, 'and I'm only a few miles from where I was born.'

They followed the housekeeper through endless corridors until they reached a small staircase tucked away in a narrow passage. They climbed to the second floor before they were finally ushered into a vast attic with overhead lighting and a row of windows overlooking the front of the house. The severe woman who had interviewed them was waiting and they spent the next hour or so being led along the long tables where the repair work was being done. A cup of tea would have been nice, reflected Julia, being shown the wall tapestry she would be working on.

There wasn't much of the afternoon left. The half-dozen women around her began to pack up presently, and thankfully she and Jenny were shown the way to a room on the ground floor where tea was waiting. It was more than tea; there were eggs and ham, several kinds of bread, butter, pots of jam, a splendid cake and a great pot of tea. Julia, eating with a splendid appetite, wondered if this was the last meal of the day, for it was almost six o'clock.

As they got up from the table one of the women said in a friendly voice, 'You're new, aren't you? There's sandwiches and hot drinks about eight o'clock. Some of us live in the village but two of us live here in the house.'

It was going to be all right, Julia decided, going sleepily to her bed later that evening. Everyone was friendly, she had a pleasant room, good, wholesome food and she would be working at something she enjoyed doing. Nevertheless she cried herself to sleep, and her last thoughts were of Gerard. He would forget her, of course. Probably by the time she got back to London he would have gone back to Holland and got married into the bargain.

The Professor went about his work in his usual calm manner. For the moment there was nothing to be done; first he had to find out where Julia had gone.

It was some days before he saw Ruth and enquired casually as to whether she had heard from Julia. And Ruth blushed because she was longing to tell him where Julia was, but a promise was a promise...

'She's very happy...'

'Splendid. What kind of a job is it?'

There would be no harm in telling him that. 'Repairing old tapestries.'

'And where is she?'

Ruth blushed again. 'She asked me not to tell you and I promised.'

'Then I won't bother you. I hope she will settle down and enjoy life. How fortunate that she heard of something so soon after coming back.'

'Oh, it wasn't sudden; she told me she'd applied for the job while she was still in Holland with Mrs Beckett—she saw it advertised in a magazine.'

Now he had one or two clues. He said casually, 'And how are Monica and George getting on? Will you be visiting them now that you're nicely settled in here?'

So Ruth told him all about the new bathrooms and the central heating in the vicarage, pleased that she had given nothing away about Julia.

It was the following day before the Professor had the leisure to phone Mrs Beckett. He listened patiently to her detailed account of her progress and when she paused for breath he asked, 'Nanny, which magazines do you read?'

'Now there's a funny question,' observed Mrs Beckett. 'English ones, of course, they get sent each week.' She named them and added, 'Why do you want to know, Mr Gerard?'

'Do any of them advertise jobs?'

'Not all of them. The *Lady* does—pages and pages of them.'

'Nanny, have you heard from Julia?'

Mrs Beckett looked out of the window and smiled. 'Well, yes, bless the dear child. Sent me a long letter but forgot the address. Got a lovely job, she says, embroidering and suchlike. The post mark was Carlisle. Seems a long way from home, but I dare say she was visiting friends.'

His 'Probably' was non-committal, and she put down the phone with another smile. The path of true love never did run smooth, she informed a rather surprised Miss Thrisp.

True enough. But that wasn't going to deter the Professor from his own particular path. His secretary was bidden to obtain back copies of the *Lady* and he searched the advertisements until he found what he sought...

Life was very different for Julia now. The work was interesting and she enjoyed it; the other women were friendly and they were well looked after. There was a vast park to walk in when she had finished work in the evening, and an estate Land Rover took the staff to the village or Haltwhistle when they were free. All the same, she was lonely. It was a splendid job, she told herself. The country around was vast and lonely and very much to her liking, and although she didn't regret leaving London it was impossible to forget Gerard. She consoled herself with the thought that he would have forgotten her by now, but that couldn't stop her loving him.

She took to getting up early and walking in the park before breakfast. It was peaceful there: birds singing, distant sounds coming from the Home Farm, subdued noise from the great house waking to another day. It was such a vast place that she had only seen a little of it, and nothing of its owners.

She had been there for almost two weeks when a particularly splendid morning got her out of bed earlier than usual. She showered and dressed and drank her early-morning tea and let herself out of her room. There was no one about and she crossed the courtyard and went into the parkland beyond. Part of it was wooded, and there was a lake which dribbled into a small stream, and on such a morning it was a delight to the eye.

She wandered along and presently sat down on a tree stump, allowing her thoughts to wander too. She supposed that sooner or later she would go back to London, find herself a small flat and put her talents to good use. At least she would have a reference, and there were museums and art galleries and private houses who would employ her. And, although she might never see the Professor, she would be near him...

A cheerful 'Good morning' got her to her feet. A man was coming towards her, a young man with a pleasant rugged face. There were two dogs with him who crowded round her, tails wagging.

'You'll be one of the needlewomen,' said the man cheerfully. 'I heard Mother saying that there were one or two new ladies.' He held out a hand. 'Menton— Colin Menton.'

Julia smiled at him, warmed by his friendliness.

'Gracey,' she said in her turn. 'Julia. How do you do?'

They shook hands and he asked, 'Where are you from?'

'London.'

'You're a long way from home. Do you like it here? It is really rather different.'

'I didn't live in a very nice part of London; this seems like heaven.'

'It is.' They were strolling back towards the house. 'But it's not to everyone's taste—too quiet.'

'That's why it's heaven.' They had reached the courtyard. 'I must go.'

'Nice meeting you. Perhaps we shall see each other again. Do you go walking each morning?'

'Well, yes.'

'Then we'll meet again.'

She thought about him while she stitched patiently. It had been pleasant to talk to someone of her own age; the other needlewomen were really friendly, and she got on well with them, but they were twice her age and Jenny went to her home when she was free. Julia explored when she was free. Haltwhistle was near enough for her half-day expeditions. It was a small market town with a fine church, and she sent picture postcards to Ruth and Monica, quite forgetting that they might be shown to the Professor.

One day she got a lift to the small village of Greenhead. The road running through it was close to the Roman Wall and she walked for miles until she found a side road which took her back to Haltwhistle and eventually back to the estate. It was a long walk and she enjoyed every minute of it. She didn't feel lonely in the country and she had her thoughts of Gerard to keep her company.

She had done the right thing, she told herself; she had no intention of mooning after a man who hardly noticed her. Once or twice she had thought they could have been friends, but that had been a flash in the pan. And anyway there was always the possibility that Gerard would have gone back to Holland.

The thought of never seeing him again was unbearable, but she would have to learn to bear it and it would surely be easier as time passed. There was always the chance that they might meet... She would stay at the estate for as long as there was work for her, and then she would have to decide her future and what better place in which to do it than this remote countryside?

She wrote cheerful letters to Ruth and Monica, though both of them were mystified as to why she shouldn't want anyone to know where she was. But since she seemed so happy and content with the job, and they were both fully occupied with their own lives, they didn't pursue the matter further. Perhaps if the Professor had mentioned her on one of his infrequent visits they might have given it more thought...

A few days later Julia met Colin Menton again. The day's work was finished and she was crossing the courtyard to go to her room. It was late afternoon and still warm. She would go for a walk before supper and then write letters.

He met her halfway. 'Hello, finished work for the day? I don't suppose you feel like a walk? I'm going to the other end of the park to see if the trees we planted are doing well.' He smiled at her. 'Do say yes.'

Julia laughed. 'Well, all right, yes.'

The park was vast, merging now and again into fields of rough grass. Close to the house the gardens had been skilfully laid out, and there was a lake bordered by trees, but presently they followed a path into the trees on the edge of the park. It was pleasant walking and they found plenty to talk about. He begged her to call him Colin and told her that he'd been spending a month or two at his home before taking up a post abroad as an agricultural adviser. 'I shall be getting married before we go,' he confided.

Julia sensed a wish to talk about his fiancée. 'Is she pretty?' she asked.

The rest of their walk was taken up with a detailed description of his fiancée's perfections, and as they neared the house again he said awkwardly, 'Have I been boring you? Only I do like to talk about her.'

'Well, of course you do. She sounds a perfect dear, as well as being so pretty. I'm sure you'll both be very happy. How much longer will you be here?'

'Ten days. We're being married from her home in Wiltshire. We didn't want a big wedding, but you know what mothers are.'

They were standing in the courtyard. 'I enjoyed our walk. I suppose you wouldn't like to drive over to Hexham? I have to see someone there but it shouldn't take too long. There is a splendid abbey there that you might like to visit if you're interested.'

'I should like that. I get two half-days in the week—Tuesday and Thursday, both in the morning.'

'Next Tuesday? It's no distance—fifteen miles or

so. If we left around nine o'clock we could have coffee before I see this fellow. You can look round and visit the abbey and I'll meet you for lunch.'

'I have to be back at work by two o'clock.'

'Easily done. We can lunch early.'

Julia agreed; the prospect of an outing was inviting and there might be time to do some shopping.

Jenny, working beside her on the worn tapestry they were patiently repairing, gave her a quick glance as they started to stitch.

'How are you getting on?' she wanted to know. 'This is a grand job. If we ever get our time off together you must come home with me. You've no idea how marvellous it is to be back with the family. You look perky. Have you made any friends?'

Julia nodded. 'And I walk miles—I love walking and the country is beautiful. I met Mr Menton one morning. He's offered me a lift to Hexham—I'd like to see the abbey and do some shopping.'

'Young Mr Menton? He's nice—getting married soon, did you know?'

'Yes, he told me about his fiancée and the job he's going to. He's leaving very shortly. Will the family go to the wedding? What happens here if they do? Will we still be open to the public?'

'I shouldn't think so. We'll be told, I suppose.' Jenny gave Julia an enquiring look. 'It's likely that there will be enough work for us until early next year. There are the curtains in the drawing room to mend and that wall tapestry in the hall. It'll be cold here after London. Will you stay?'

'Why not? Unless I have a good reason to go back

to London. I have two married sisters; they might have babies or need me for something or other.'

She spoke cheerfully but, much though she liked her surroundings, the prospect of being there for almost another six months was daunting. After all she had money now, enough to get a mortgage on a small flat—not necessarily in London—and find work. She choked back dismay at the prospect. She was letting herself drift; she who had never been faint-hearted in her life before.

That evening she borrowed an atlas. She mustn't be too far away from Ruth and Monica, but far away enough from London and Gerard. She made a list of likely towns and went to bed feeling that she had at last begun to organise her future.

And on Tuesday afternoon, bending over her stitching, she went over the trip to Hexham. It had been a success. She and Colin had fallen into an easy friendship and there had never been a lack of something to talk about during the short drive. They had had coffee before parting, and she had spent a happy morning looking round the abbey and then looking at the shops, buying some books and other small items on a list she had made. They had met at a pleasant old pub and had had an early lunch before driving back. It had been a pleasant morning and she would miss his cheerful face and casual friendliness. He was leaving on Thursday, and she had said that she would say goodbye to him before she set off on a walk before starting work that afternoon.

He was to leave early, but she had breakfast before she went out to the yard. He had already said goodbye to his family and his car, an Aston Martin, was there, with him in the driving seat.

Julia lent over to shake his hand. 'Go carefully, and have a lovely wedding.'

'Oh, we will. I'm glad we met, Julia. I hope you will have a lovely wedding to some lucky chap one day.' He kissed her cheek just as the Professor drove the Rolls into the yard.

CHAPTER SEVEN

JULIA straightened up with a laugh—and saw the Professor's car. The wild rush of delight at the sight of him turned at once to a mixture of panic and bad temper. Panic because he might have bad news of her sisters, and temper because she was wearing an old skirt and a cotton top, suitable for a walk in the country but not for meeting him of all people.

She waved in answer to Colin's wave, and watched the Professor get out of his car and come towards her. She would have liked to have run to meet him, but something in his leisurely approach stopped her. Yet when he reached her his, 'Hello, Julia,' was uttered in the mildest of voices.

She asked breathlessly, 'How did you know I was here?' She frowned. 'I asked Ruth...'

'Who told me nothing. But rest assured that I am quite capable of finding you if I wish to do so.'

'So why did you?'

'There would be no point in telling you that at the moment. I'm glad to see that you have found friends. Or should I say a friend.' His voice was silky.

'Colin?' She wanted to shake his calm. 'Oh, yes, we've had some pleasant walks. He is the son of the house.' She added, without much truth, 'We've seen quite a lot of the surrounding country—Hadrian's Wall...'

When he didn't speak she asked uneasily, 'Do you have friends in this part of the world?'

'Colleagues at the hospital in Carlisle.'

'Oh, you're doing something there?'

He didn't answer, only asked, 'When do you work?'

'From nine in the morning until five o'clock. We get breaks for meals and two half-days.' She added defiantly, 'I'm loving it.'

'And is this a half-day?'

She said Yes so reluctantly that he smiled.

'Then perhaps you will spend it with me? We could drive to Hadrian's Wall and have a walk and an early lunch. When must you start work?'

'Two o'clock.'

'An hour or two in the fresh air and a brisk walk will do you good.'

'I go walking each morning...'

He said smoothly, 'Ah, yes, but now that you will be walking alone it is never as inviting, is it? Go and do something to your hair. I'll wait here. Ten minutes?'

'I haven't said I would come...'

He smiled and her heart turned over. 'But you will!'

She went to her room then and got into a cotton jersey dress, and did her hair again and made up her face nicely, all the while telling herself that she was mad to be doing it. On the other hand, he would soon be gone again, back to London. Surely an hour or so in his company wouldn't make any difference to her resolve not to see him again. She wondered briefly how he had discovered where she was... She didn't waste time thinking about it; half-days were precious, and every minute of them had to be enjoyed. She hurried back to the yard and found the Professor leaning against his car, talking to Jenny, on her way to start her morning's work.

'Lucky you,' she called cheerfully. 'Don't forget the time, though in your shoes I would.'

Julia tried not to see the wink which accompanied the remark.

The Professor stowed her into the Rolls and drove away, embarking at the same time on a casual conversation which put her instantly at ease. She reflected that this unexpected meeting should have bothered her, but it hadn't. It seemed the most natural thing in the world that Gerard should have appeared out of the blue, as it were, and that they should be spending the morning together as if they were old friends. But, of course, it wasn't that at all; he had felt the need of company and had an hour or so to spare.

The Professor glanced at her puzzled face and smiled to himself. Just for once Julia had lost her tongue.

He took her to Brampton, not many miles away, gave her coffee at the hotel there, parked the car, booked a table for lunch and marched her off briskly. Hadrian's Wall was no distance, and when they reached it they walked beside it. It was quiet and the countryside was empty; the road was nearby but there was little traffic, and it was cool enough to make walking a pleasure. And they talked.

It was surprising how easy it was to talk to him, thought Julia, discussing her future, her doubts and problems until at a certain moment she stopped abruptly. She was a fool, telling him all this; he wouldn't be in the least interested. He might even be bored.

'Do you know this part of the world?' she wanted to know.

'Not well enough.' He had seen her sudden reluctance to talk about herself and so slipped easily into a casual discussion of the country around them. Presently she was lulled into the idea that he hadn't been listening, had shown no sign of interest. She had been a fool, telling him of her plans when she had made up her mind not to see him again. She supposed that being in love made one foolish...

Back at the hotel they had lunch in a delightful restaurant, its windows overlooking a well-kept garden. The place was half full and the service friendly. Julia, hungry after their walk, made a splendid meal. The food was well cooked and plentiful on the estate, but the food set before her now was something of a treat: game soup, a meal in itself, roast beef with Yorkshire pudding to dream of, roasted parsnips, crisp and golden brown, and a crême brulée which melted in the mouth.

'I'm not going to offer you wine,' said the Professor, 'or you'll droop over your curtains!' So they drank tonic water.

He drove her back afterwards, making casual small talk, and back in the court yard, when she would have uttered her carefully rehearsed thank-you speech, he said abruptly, 'I'm glad you enjoyed the morning. You must get Colin to take you again while the weather is good.'

Julia could think of nothing to say but, 'Yes', and

watched him drive away while all she wanted to say
crowded her tongue unuttered. Perhaps it was just as
well, she thought unhappily. For a short time she had
thought that perhaps he had sought her out because
he had wanted to see her again, but that wasn't so;
he had had a morning to spare and had used it to
make sure that she was all right so that he could tell
Ruth. It was a lowering thought...

The Professor drove himself back to London deep in
thought. Julia had been glad to see him, he had seen
the look on her face, but had the delight been at the
sight of him or because he was someone from home?
And this man, this young man, reflected Gerard,
deeply aware that at thirty-six he could no longer be
considered young. Though a man of no conceit, he
was aware that he could make her fall in love with
him—but he had no intention of doing that; she must
learn to love him of her own free will. That they were
meant for each other was something he never
doubted.

He didn't think that she was happy; she liked her
work and the surroundings in which she lived but she
was sad about something. There was nothing he could
do for the moment only have patience.

He phoned Ruth when he got back and gave her a
reassuring account of Julia.

'I suppose he went to the Carlisle hospital,' she told
Thomas, 'and discovered where she was.'

And Thomas, who knew better, agreed with her.

A week or two went by. The weather was unusually
warm and dry, even in the north of the country, and

sitting for long hours stitching was tiring. Julia, taking her solitary early morning walks, made plans for the future and then discarded them. There was a rumour that once the tapestry they were working on was finished they would be asked to work at the town-house the family owned in London. The local women wouldn't go, but Jenny and she might be offered work there. That wouldn't do. Forgetting Gerard was harder than she had thought it would be. And how could she forget him when she loved him? The only thing to do was to go away, as far as possible...

She wrote cheerful letters to Ruth and Monica and scanned their replies for a mention of the Professor, but it was as though he had never existed.

It was some time after four o'clock in the afternoon when the fire broke out. A sightseer, disregarding the 'No Smoking' notices, had lighted a cigarette and tossed the still burning match to one side. It had fallen onto the curtains shrouding the state dining room windows. Dry as dust, and fragile with age, they had smouldered unnoticed for some minutes and then suddenly burst into flames which had swept across the room and into an adjoining salon. From there it leapt from wall-panelling to tapestries, to chairs and tables, through the wide archway and into the music room beyond...

It was a large, rambling mansion, and there was no one in that wing when the fire started. By the time the alarm was raised it had spread, burning the telephone cable and the fire alarm which connected it to the police station at Haltwhistle.

There was a certain amount of panic and great confusion, so that no one remembered that up on the fourth floor, under the roof, there were seven women, stitching...

Sounds from outside the house were muted in the attics; cars and coaches arriving with visitors were sounds so frequent that they were disregarded, as were the voices. The windows at the front of the house were kept shut on open days, since fumes from the cars might harm the delicate materials they were working upon, but that afternoon Julia's ear caught another sound: voices raised in alarm—more than alarm, terror: And seconds later she smelled the smoke. She went to a window and looked out and saw one wing of the house in flames, people getting into cars and buses and a confused mass of those who didn't know what to do...

By then the other women had left their work and joined her at the window.

'We'd better make haste and get out.' One of the women from the village, older than the rest, spoke urgently. 'We're quite safe if we go down the back stairs.' And indeed the fire was reassuringly distant from them.

But when they reached the second landing it was to find the staircase below already alight.

So far there had been no panic, they weren't women to do that, but now the sight of the smoke and the flames creeping around the staircase on the floor below shattered their calm. Someone screamed.

'The garden door at the back of the house—there's a small staircase...'

Someone told the screamer to be quiet, in a voice rendered hoarse by anger and fright, and they ran through the main part of the house along corridors and passages Julia had never seen before and found the staircase. It was still intact, but the floor below was well alight.

Julia caught one of the older women by the arm. 'If we go back to the attics we can break the windows—there's a narrow parapet, isn't there? Someone will see us; there will be a fire escape...'

The woman nodded. 'We're going back,' she shouted above the panicky voices. 'They'll get us off the roof.'

They went back the way they had come, and although there was a smell of burning and wisps of smoke and a great deal of noise the fire was out of sight. And once back in the attics they set about breaking the glass in the windows at the front of the house, shouting for help as they did so.

The fire had spread to the centre of the house by now, and there were a great many people running to and fro, but the noise of the fire carried away the voices of the women in the attic and no one saw them.

It was Julia who picked up a stool and hurled it over the parapet, and within seconds they were all tossing anything they could carry into the sweep below. And now they could see upturned faces, waving arms, people running and the heartening sight of the first of the fire engines belting up the drive. The third floor was alight now and the hoses were turned on to it. If the fire could be halted there, thought Julia, we'd have a good chance of getting out. She said so, loudly, and the little band of terrified women took heart.

It was five minutes—the longest five minutes of her life, reflected Julia later—before the fire rescue team arrived, and another five minutes saw the first of them being edged over the parapet and into the arms of the fireman perched on the end of the fire escape. In unspoken consent, the women who had children were the first to be rescued, then the two elderly ladies who were married to estate workers, and lastly Jenny and Julia.

And Julia, waiting alone in a blur of held-back terror, allowed herself to scream—for there was no one to hear above the roar of the flames below. She felt better once she had screamed; she had nothing to be frightened about now, the firemen would be back for her in a few minutes. Only she wished with her whole heart that Gerard was there beside her telling her not to worry…

The attic was filling with smoke when she was helped over the parapet.

The Professor was home early. He went to his study with Wilf and Robbie, closely followed by Mrs Potts and the tea tray, and sat down at his desk. He had a good deal of paperwork to do, and notes for a lecture to write. He drank his tea, gave his dogs the biscuits and turned to the pile of papers on his desk. But before picking up his pen, he turned on the radio.

Just in time for a news flash that an estate in the north of England was on fire. No casualties had been reported so far, said the voice, but it was feared that there might be people trapped in the house.

The Professor's instinct was to leap from his chair into his car and drive north within seconds. Instead he picked up the phone and dialled the hospital; Thomas was still on duty. He didn't waste words.

'I'm flying up within half an hour,' he told Thomas. 'Tell Ruth that I will bring Julia back here.'

'You're sure it's where Julia is?'

'They gave the name on the radio.'

The rush hour hadn't started. The Professor, as good as his word, left his house within minutes, outwardly calm, and made for the airport. He concentrated on flying, firmly keeping other thoughts at bay.

Almost at his journey's end, after picking up a hire car, he could see the glow of the fire ahead of him, and shortly after he turned into the drive leading to the house. He was stopped before he was halfway there.

'Sorry, sir, you can't go any further. Can I help?'

'Indeed you can. My future wife works here. She would have been on the top floor. I've come to take her back home.'

At the officer's look of enquiry, he said 'London. I've flown up. I'm a surgeon at one of the hospitals there.'

'Then you'd best find her. There's a rare old muddle checking everyone's out of the building, and quite a few have been taken off to hospital for a check-up or been taken home—local folk.' He nodded at the Professor. 'I'll phone through.'

The Professor drove on, parked the hire car and got out. The sweep in front of the house was crowded with people: firemen, police, estate workers and people from the village. The officer he spoke to was helpful; everyone had been got out and had been sent home, if they lived in the village, or into hospital at Carlisle... It was an elderly man standing near them who interrupted.

'Not all of 'em,' he said. 'There's one of the sewing ladies over at my place with the missus. Not from hereabouts, she isn't, and got nowhere to go.' He added, 'I'm the head gardener here.'

He glanced at the Professor. 'You'd best go and take a look. It's the end cottage, on its own.' He waved an arm. Tell the missus I sent you.'

The Professor thanked him and made his way through the throng, holding down his impatience and anxiety with a firm hand. When he reached the cottage he paused for a moment as an elderly woman came to the door. She was a sensible woman, who listened to his quick explanation and told him to go into the kitchen. 'If it's a girl called Julia, it's her,' she told him softly. 'She's not hurt, but she was the last to be rescued and it's shook her up badly.'

He thanked her quietly and pushed open the kitchen door. Julia was sitting in a chair by the old-fashioned stove, and when she looked up at him the Professor forgot that he was tired, hungry and thirsty. He would have flown ten times the distance he had to see that look on her face.

He spoke quickly, because he could see that she was struggling with tears.

'It's all right, my dear. We'll go home just as soon as I've let someone know that you are in safe hands.' He smiled down at her with the kindliness of an old family friend or elder brother.

She found her voice. 'Gerard, oh, Gerard. I've been so terrified and I didn't know what to do—and then you came...'

She gave him a lop-sided, watery small smile, and

perhaps it was as well that the gardener's wife came in then.

'You could do with a cup of tea. You'll just have to see the police—the one who got the others sorted out is in that car with the blue light.' She turned to Julia. 'You do know this gentleman, miss?'

Julia nodded. 'Oh, yes, we're...' She stopped and added, 'He knows my family too; he'll take me home.'

'Then I'll boil the kettle, sir, and you come back as soon as you can. I dare say you've got a way to go.'

The Professor only smiled and went away, and Julia said, 'London.'

'You mean to say he's come up from London?'

'No, no. He sometimes comes to Carlisle, to the hospital—he's a surgeon.'

'Well, that's good fortune indeed. Here's your tea. Drink it hot; you're still all of a shake.'

Which was true enough. She had drunk half of it when the Professor came back. He drank his own tea, thanked the gardener's wife and walked Julia to the car. He had an arm around her and she was glad of it, for her legs felt like jelly. When they reached the car, he picked her up and popped her in, and fetched a rug from the boot and wrapped her in it. And all this with the air of an elder brother...

The car was warm and comfortable and she closed her eyes, only opening them when a police officer put his head through the open window.

'You're Miss Julia Gracey? I'm just checking that everything is OK.'

She managed a smile. 'Yes, that's me, and this is

Professor van der Maes, who is a friend of my family.'

He nodded. 'There'll be someone round to see you at home, just to make sure that you are fit and well—get the record straight.' He grinned at her. 'You had a lucky escape, miss.' He turned to the professor. 'Safe journey, sir.'

Gerard got into the hire car and drove back down the drive and on to the road. They would have to stop on the way to the airport. He was tired and hungry, and Julia, even if she slept, would need a break and food. He glanced sideways at her, cocooned in the rug.

'We should be back in a couple of hours. We will stop on the way for a hot drink and something to eat. Are you all right?'

He sounded reassuringly normal. 'Yes, thank you. Oh, Gerard, how fortunate that you were here—I mean, at the hospital in Carlisle.' When he didn't answer she said, 'You were there, weren't you? I mean, how else could you have come so quickly?'

'I heard the news when I got home...'

She peered at him over the rug. 'You came all the way from London?' Her voice was an unbelieving squeak.

'Yes. Now go to sleep, Julia.'

And, while she was still feeling indignant about that, she did.

The professor looked at Julia's sleeping face. She was pale and smelled of smoke and her hair was in a tangle, but she was here, beside him, safe and sound. He kissed her grubby cheek and drove on.

At a service station he woke her gently. 'I'll get us

tea and something to eat,' he told her. 'But first I'll walk you to the facilities.'

Julia, feeling better, was soon shovelled back into the car and told to stay awake.

The tea was hot and sweet and there were sandwiches, cut thick and filled with corned beef. They ate and drank in comfortable silence, the quiet dark around them.

Later, halfway through their short flight, Julia said, 'Would you mind if I went to sleep again for a little while? I'm tired.'

He had expected that, and had already tucked a rug round her. He held his own tiredness at bay while he considered plans and discarded them. Once Julia had recovered from her fright and shock she would probably disappear again; the last thing he wanted was for her to feel beholden to him.

In London, he had to stop once more. 'I'm going to be sick,' said Julia, suddenly awake. He stopped, hauled her briskly out of the car and held her while she heaved and choked and then burst into tears. He mopped her face, popped her back into the car, tucked her up once more and gave her a handful of paper tissues. 'You'll feel better now, try and rest again.'

She closed her eyes but she didn't sleep. She thought about him. He had been quick and gentle and matter-of-fact and impersonal, and she sensed a professional remoteness. And why should it be otherwise? she reflected sadly. The only times they met hadn't been because they had wanted to but by force of circumstances. *Why* had he come all the way from London? She was too sleepy to think about that, but just as she was dozing off she muttered, 'Ruth would have been worried—and he likes her and Thomas.'

The Professor smiled to himself. It was as good a reason as any.

It was late when he stopped before his house. He had phoned before they had left the estate and asked Mrs Potts to get a room ready for Julia. 'And go to bed,' he had told her, 'for we shall be back after midnight.'

Julia was awake again. He got out of the car and, with an arm round her, opened his front door. There was a wall lamp alight and as they went in Mrs Potts, cosily wrapped in a woolly dressing gown, came down the staircase.

'There you are,' she observed, 'and tired to death, I'll be bound, sir. Now, just you go to the kitchen and eat and drink what's there while I take miss upstairs. She'll have a nice warm bath and bed, and a glass of warm milk.' She nodded her head. 'And you'll go to bed too, sir.'

The Professor smiled at her. 'You're an angel, Mrs Potts. Have you had any sleep yourself?'

'Bless you, sir, I went to bed early, seeing as how things were.'

He picked up Julia and carried her upstairs and laid her on the bed in a small bedroom.

'Don't go,' said Julia, clutching his arm. 'I haven't thanked you.' She sounded meek and tearful, and later she would feel ashamed of herself for being so silly.

'We will talk in the morning,' said the Professor bracingly, and went away. Next she heard Mrs Potts's soft voice. 'Now, we'll have these clothes off you. You just sit there while I help you. Then a nice bath, and I'll wash your hair, and then bed and a good sound sleep. The Professor's going to bed too and you can both have a nice chat in the morning.'

So Julia was bathed and shampooed, and all the while Mrs Potts talked in a soothing voice and finally tucked her up in bed and told her to go to sleep. Which she did.

She woke to hear dogs barking and the muted sounds of a household getting ready for the day and, reassured, went back to sleep.

It was mid-morning when she sat up in bed, feeling perfectly well again, and found Mrs Potts standing by the bed with a breakfast tray.

'Oh, I could have got up for breakfast,' said Julia. 'I've given you so much trouble already and I feel fine…'

Mrs Potts arranged the tray on a bed table. 'Now just eat your breakfast, Miss Gracey. Your sister will be here with some clothes for you presently.'

'Ruth? How did she know that I was here?'

'Why, the Professor phoned her before he went to the hospital this morning. She's to stay for lunch.'

'Lunch? What's the time, Mrs Potts?'

'A little after ten o'clock.'

'The Professor said he'd see me in the morning. He's still here?'

'Lor' bless you, Miss, he's been gone these past two hours.' Mrs Potts shook her head. 'There's no stopping him. A couple of hours' sleep and he's off again. I'm to tell you he'll see you some time.'

Julia drank her tea and swallowed tears with it. 'Yes, of course. I've given him a lot of trouble. I'll go back with my sister after lunch. Is there somewhere I could write him a note?'

'I'll have pen and paper ready for you,' promised Mrs Potts, and left Julia to finish a breakfast which tasted of sawdust. He had gone to a great deal of trouble to rescue her, but now that was accomplished he would forget her—a momentary nuisance in his ordered life.

'But I'm not going to cry about it,' said Julia, and ate the breakfast she no longer wanted, then got up and showered. Wrapped in a voluminous dressing gown produced by Mrs Potts, she went downstairs, where she was shown into a small, cosily furnished room. There was a small writing desk with paper and pen set ready for her.

'Your sister will be here presently,' said Mrs Potts comfortably, and left her to write her note.

Not an easy thing to do, Julia discovered. She had to make several attempts before she was satisfied, but she hoped that her warm thanks coupled with the assumption that she was unlikely to see him—his work—her intention to leave London as soon as possible—would strike the right note. She had just sealed the envelope when Ruth arrived, bringing clothes and agog to hear exactly what had happened.

When Julia had finished telling her everything she said, 'I didn't know anything about it until Gerard phoned Thomas to say that he had found you and that you were safe…'

Julia said slowly, 'I thought he had come because you were worried about me?'

'No, no. Thomas told me that Gerard phoned him

around half past four—he'd heard a newsflash about the fire. He was on the point of leaving.'

She saw the look on Julia's face and said quickly, 'You'll stay with us, of course, love, until you decide what you want to do.'

Julia said slowly, 'Would you mind if I went to Monica for a while?'

'No, of course not. It will be quiet there; you will have time to think.'

Something Julia didn't want to do, for she would only think of Gerard, who had rescued her and left a laconic message that he would see her some time. Well, that was something she could deal with. If she went to Monica he could forget her, something he must be wanting to do, only fate seemed intent on throwing her in his path.

They had their lunch, thanked Mrs Potts for her kindness and took a taxi to Ruth's home. Thomas was at the hospital and Julia seized the opportunity to phone Monica and invite herself to stay. 'Just for a week. I won't be in the way, but it would be nice to have a few days while I make up my mind what I'll do.'

'Come for as long as you like,' said Monica largely. 'No one will bother you. It must have been horrible, Julia, and so far away. You must have been glad to see Gerard.'

'Yes,' said Julia. 'I was. He's been very kind...'

'More than kind,' said Monica dryly. 'Come when you like, Julia; there's a room ready for you. The nearest station is Cullompton. George will meet you with the car.'

Thomas came home presently. He was glad to see

her, and wanted to know about the fire—and never mentioned Gerard. She said in a carefully casual voice, 'I haven't seen Gerard since we got back here. I hope he wasn't too tired...'

'Gerard's never tired,' said Thomas. 'He's done a day's work and he's dining out this evening with the widow of one of his patients who has been angling for him for some time.'

Well, thought Julia peevishly, I don't need to waste any concern on the man. I hope she catches him and leads him a simply horrible life. She smiled brilliantly at her brother-in-law and wished she could go and shut herself somewhere dark and lonely and cry her heart out.

And Ruth made it worse by observing that Olivia Travis was one of the most beautiful women she had ever met. 'If I were a man I'd fall in love with her the moment I saw her.'

Thomas grunted, which could have meant anything.

Julia stayed for three days at Ruth's. She had to buy clothes and be interviewed by someone from the police, who assured her that they merely wished to be sure that she was quite unharmed and safe with her family. And each morning when she woke she wondered if she would see the Professor. But he didn't come. Nor did Thomas speak of him. She told herself that she was glad. He could at least have acknowledged her note, though. Perhaps he hadn't read it. His secretary might have put it with the junk mail and all the invitations which he didn't wish to accept.

On the third day she made arrangements to go to Monica. Ruth asked worriedly, 'Will you stay for a while, love? Come back here when you want to.'

'I'm being a worry for them,' Julia told herself as she got ready for bed. 'I must find something somewhere and settle down.'

Perhaps in some small town in the West Country. A small flat—she could rent one—or a shop. She had money enough; there was no reason why she shouldn't make a pleasant life for herself. She might even marry...

Out of the question, of course. She loved Gerard and no one else would do.

Up until the very last minute, until the train was leaving the station, she had the forlorn hope that she would see Gerard. But there was no sign of him. He'd be in Holland, thought Julia despairingly, and then, as the train swept past the suburbs and through green fields and trees, That's it, she told herself. You're going to forget him just as he's forgotten you. You're wasting your life hankering after a person who doesn't care a straw for you.

After which heartening speech she picked up the magazine she had bought and began to read it. It was full of artfully posed teenagers wearing what looked like fancy dress costumes, and they were all painfully bony, with sharp elbows and jutting collarbones. Julia felt fat and almost middle-aged just looking at them. She handed the magazine over to a young woman who had been peering at it from the opposite seat and then looked out of the window. The country looked lovely and she felt a sudden surge of interest in the future.

You never know what's round the corner, thought Julia.

CHAPTER EIGHT

GEORGE, driving Julia away from Cullompton station, didn't bother her with questions. He thought that she looked tired and, despite her bright chatter, unhappy. He would leave the questions to Monica, he decided.

Monica was waiting for them with a string of questions and they had a cheerful lunch together.

'I'll take you over the house again, now that we've had the alterations done,' said Monica. 'It's far too large for us, of course, but we love it. And now we've got central heating and the plumbing works, it's easy to run.'

They had gone to Julia's bedroom after lunch and Monica was sitting on the bed while Julia unpacked.

'Is Ruth all right? And Thomas? And have you seen the Professor since you got back? What a man—going all that way to fetch you home. I expect he must have seen how worried Ruth was, but it was a noble thing to do, especially as you don't like each other much.'

Julia had her head in a drawer. 'Yes, it was. I haven't seen him since, though, but I didn't expect to.'

'Ruth told me that there's a beautiful woman lurking!'

'Yes.' Julia emerged rather red in the face. 'I had a present for you, but of course I lost it in the fire. Perhaps we could find something to take its place.

This really is a lovely old house, isn't it? Ruth's house is nice, too…'

Monica said concernedly, 'But you haven't a home, love. We do worry about you.'

Julia closed her case and put it tidily under the bed. 'Well, don't. I know exactly what I want to do. Leave London, for a start, and settle in a town between the two of you. I'll rent a flat to start with, and then find a small shop with living space. I shall sell everything to do with needlework and knitting and embroidery. While I'm here, if you don't mind, I shall take a look at some of the small towns round and about. I can hire a car. I know I haven't driven for years but I can't have forgotten how.'

Monica said suddenly, 'Do you ever wish that you'd married Oscar?'

Julia laughed. 'Monica, you must be joking! I'm happy as I am. "Footloose and fancy-free"—isn't that what someone or other wrote?'

Monica laughed too, and didn't believe a word of it.

It was delightful living in the country. The village was a large one with a widespread parish, and Monica and George made her more than welcome, but after a few days she declared her intention of exploring the surrounding countryside with an eye to the future.

Honiton seemed as good a place to start as any. A small market town straddling the main road from London to the West, it was famous for its lace-making and antiques shops, but she discarded it reluctantly. It was too near Monica and too far from Ruth. It needed to be somewhere between her sisters and far enough away from both of them so as not to encroach on their lives. She pored over maps and guidebooks and, sitting one morning with Monica in the garden asked, 'Where's Stourhead?'

'North of Yeovil. Not on a main road but easy to get at. It's a lovely place; we went there a month or so ago. Heavenly gardens and a Palladian house full of treasures.'

'There's an ad in your local newspaper. Guides for the house and people to repair and refurbish the furniture and the hangings. I know I want to start up on my own, but it looks rather inviting.'

She could see Monica's look of uncertainty and knew what she was thinking: that she was wasting time, drifting from one job to another, that she should settle down and make a secure future for herself—that was if she didn't marry, and that didn't seem likely.

Monica said worriedly, 'Yes, that might be a good idea. While you were there you might scout around and find a suitable shop in one of the small towns not too far away. There's Sherborne—the most likely, I should think. Yeovil is nearby, too, but that's quite large—too large for the kind of shop you're thinking of, I imagine. There's Warminster and there's Gillingham and Shaftesbury, but I'm not sure if you could make much of a living with the kind of shop you're thinking of. I'd opt for Sherborne...'

So Julia went to Sherborne and liked what she saw there. It was an abbey town with a well-known public school and the right kind of shops. For the first time since she had returned from the north she felt enthusiastic about her future. She supposed that all this time she had been hoping that she would see Gerard

again, that he might even discover that he liked her...
But that wasn't going to be the case. Once and for all
she would forget him.

Quite sure now that she knew what she wanted to
do, she wasted no time. A visit to the town's estate
agents left her with a handful of possible shops to
buy or lease. She would strike while the iron was hot,
she decided, viewing the future through rose-coloured
spectacles. And phoned Monica to tell her that she
was going to stay the night in Sherborne and inspect
what was on offer.

'You haven't got anything with you,' Monica reminded her, so she went out and bought a cheap
nightie and a toothbrush and booked in at a quiet hotel
five minutes' walk from the town centre. It was already late afternoon, but it was a small town and she
had no trouble finding the handful of addresses. The
first three were no use at all, tucked away down side
streets, but the fourth had possibilities; it was close
to the abbey and the main shopping street, tucked in
between an antiquarian book shop and a picture gallery. Its window was small, but it was in a good state
of repair and the paintwork was fresh. She peered
through the glass door. The shop was small too, with
a tiny counter and a door behind it. The leaflet
claimed that there were living quarters too.

She reached the estate agents as they were about
to close and arranged to inspect the shop in the morning.

Momentarily inflated with a strong sense of purpose, she took herself off then to the hotel, had a
splendid dinner and slept soundly.

The shop was small but it had possibilities. There

was a little room behind it and a kitchen beyond that, and upstairs there was a bedroom and a shower and a toilet. She could, she decided, make it home without too much expense. And she could rent it on a year's lease which meant that she wouldn't need to dig too deep into her capital.

She said that she would rent it subject to a surveyor's report. 'I'll need a solicitor,' she said, 'and I'd like to take possession as soon as possible.'

She went back to Monica's that afternoon, her head full of plans and ideas. She would stay in Sherborne, get the place fit to live in, buy her stock and move in at her leisure.

Monica, told the news, nodded her head in approval. 'If that is what you want,' she said cautiously. 'I've no doubt you'll make a success of it, and you're bound to make friends—if that is what you want?'

Julia assured her that it was. Which wasn't quite true, of course. What she wanted was for Gerard to fall in love with her, marry her and live with her happily ever after, but, since that was something which wasn't going to happen, she must turn herself into a successful businesswoman.

'You'll probably meet a nice man,' said Monica.

There was no point in telling her that she already had.

'I'll have to go back to London to see the solicitor and the bank. May I stay here for a few more days while the agent gets organised at Sherborne? I'll have to sign papers and so on.'

'Stay as long as you like, love. You know you'll always be welcome here. You're not far away, and if you get a car… Could you afford that?'

'I think so. A small second-hand one.'

Several days later she went back to London and told herself that she felt relief to hear that the Professor was in Holland.

The solicitor was helpful in a cautious way; he hoped that she had thought about the drawbacks as well as the advantages of setting up a small business.

'A young lady on her own,' he said, shaking a grey head. He hadn't moved with the times, but she liked him for his fatherly concern. And the bank manager was cautious too. He would have liked her to have invested her money in something safe, so that she would have had a small steady income, and possibly lived with one or other of her sisters...

While she had been working on the estate she had picked up quite a lot of information about the wholesale firms which had supplied the materials for the work there, and it had given her some idea as to how to contact them; she intended to sell tapestries, knitting wools, embroidery silks and patterns as well as canvases and embroidery frames and anything else needful to the serious embroiderer. She would also knit herself, and sell what she knitted. She wouldn't allow herself any doubts; she had always been able to cope and this was a challenge...

She was in Ruth's sitting room, and making yet another list, when the Professor opened the door and walked in.

She sat back and gaped at him, unable to think of anything to say.

'Close your mouth, my dear,' said the Professor. 'Why are you so surprised?'

'I thought you were in Holland.' Mingled with the

delight of seeing him again was annoyance that he had sneaked in on her without warning.

He sat down and stretched out his legs, the picture of ease. 'So you're about to become a business-woman? No doubt you will be very successful, make lots of money and fulfil whatever dreams you have…'

'Don't be sarcastic,' said Julia waspishly. 'and it's none of your business.'

'You're cross. Are you not pleased to see me? I thought that we might have dinner together this evening. We could talk over old times?'

She eyed him carefully. To spend an evening with him would be a dream come true, but on the other hand she had promised herself that she would forget him. The Professor, watching her face, said in just the right off-hand manner, 'I'm going back to Holland and you are leaving London.'

In that case, reflected Julia, there would be no harm done, would there? He was making it clear that they weren't likely to see each other again.

'All right. Though I'm sure we won't find anything to talk about.'

'No? The cottage? My home in Amsterdam? Mrs Beckett? I think we may be able to sustain some kind of conversation!' He got to his feet. 'I'll call for you at half past seven.'

'Shall I dress up?'

It was the kind of remark to make him fall in love with her all over again. One moment so haughty and the next as uncertain as a schoolgirl.

He said gently, 'Something short and pretty. We'll go to Claridge's.'

The moment he had gone she ran up to her room.

There was a dress which might do. She hadn't meant to buy it but it had been so pretty: amber chiffon over a silk slip, plain, high-necked, and long-sleeved and elegant. She had bought it because it had seemed to her to stand for all the pretty clothes she had never been able to buy. Well, she would wear it—and even if she never wore it again it would be worth every penny of the money she had squandered on it.

Thomas and Ruth came in together and Julia said at once with a heightened colour, 'I've done the veg for supper and made a fruit pie. You won't mind if I go out? Gerard has asked me to dinner.'

Ruth gave Thomas an 'I told you so' look, and said, 'Oh, nice. Where's he taking you?'

'Claridge's.'

Ruth was on the point of saying, Lucky girl, but changed her mind. Having fallen in love with Thomas, just as he had fallen in love with her, without any doubts or complications, she found it hard to understand why two sensible people like the Professor and her sister could be so slow in discovering that they were meant for each other. She caught Thomas's eye and said instead, 'You could wear that amber chiffon dress…'

Studying herself in the dress later, Julia wondered if she would ever wear the dress again. She knew no one in Sherborne. It would take time to make friends, and they might not be the kind to take her anywhere as splendid as Claridge's. She would make the most of her evening, she promised herself.

She was glad that she was wearing the dress when the Professor came for her. In his sober, beautifully tailored suits he looked the epitome of the well-dressed man, but in a dinner jacket he looked magnificent.

He was standing in the hall talking to Thomas when she went down, but he turned and looked at her as she came down the stairs. 'Very pretty,' he observed, which left her doubtful as to whether he was referring to the dress or her person. She wrapped herself in the paisley shawl—the family heirloom she shared with her sisters—and bade him hello. She assured Ruth that she wouldn't be late back and went out to the car with him. She hoped that they would have the lovely time Ruth had wished them...

The streets were fairly free of traffic but their way took them through the heart of the city. Julia, mindful of good manners, made small talk from time to time, but since he replied in monosyllables she said coolly, 'You don't like me to talk?'

He glanced briefly at her. 'Why should you think that? You are determined to think the worst of me, Julia.'

Suddenly contrite, she said, 'I don't—really, I don't. You've helped me so often, even if you haven't meant to. I mean, circumstances...' She stopped. 'I've made a mess of saying that. I'm sorry. I would like us to part friends.'

'A most laudable notion. I hope that at last you are trying to overcome your initial dislike of me.'

Before she could think of an answer to that he had stopped before Claridge's entrance. And, after that, serious talk, even if she had wanted it, wasn't easy. She left the shawl in the hands of the haughty lady in charge of the cloakroom, rather deflated by the disparaging glance it was given, but her spirits were uplifted by the warm appreciation in Gerard's eyes when she joined him.

They didn't dine immediately but had their drinks in a magnificent room where a small orchestra played gentle background music. The surroundings were of a kind to make even the most uncertain girl feel cherished and beautiful, so that by the time they were seated at a table Julia felt both. Moreover, she was sitting opposite the man she loved, even if it was for the very last time. Nothing must spoil this, their final meeting…

She might be head over heels in love, but it hadn't spoiled her appetite. They had watercress soup, Dover Sole with lemon grass and tiny sautéed potatoes, and a lemon tart that was out of this world—and two glasses of champagne which gave her eyes a sparkle and her tongue a ready liveliness. She had, for the moment, quite forgotten that this was their last meeting…

The Professor, under no illusions as to that, led their talk from one thing to the other. He saw now that when Julia forgot that she didn't like him she was entirely happy in his company, so it was just a question of patience. He had no intention of forcing her hand, so he would let her have her shop for a while, and once the first flush of independence had worn off, she would turn to him. She was a darling, he reflected, but pig-headed, liable to be contrary. She must find out for herself…

So they had a delightful evening together, and it wasn't until they got back to Ruth's that Julia remembered that this really was their final meeting. All her good resolutions came tumbling back into her head, so that she said stiffly, 'Thank you for a lovely evening; I enjoyed it. I hope you will...' She began again. 'I expect you're glad to be going back to Holland. Please give my love to Mrs Beckett when you see her.' She couldn't help adding, 'Will you come back to England at all?'

'From time to time.' Indeed, he was going to Holland for a short time only, for consultations and hospital commitments there, but he had no intention of telling her that.

He got out of the car and helped her out and stood, her hand in his, looking down at her. 'A delightful evening, Julia, thank you for coming.'

She would never know what made her ask then, 'Are you going to get married?' She would have given a great deal to have unsaid her words, but they were spoken now, weren't they? And what did it matter, anyway?

The Professor studied her pink embarrassed face. He said evenly, 'Yes, that is my intention.' Idle curiosity? He wondered. Or could it be more than that?

Julia recovered herself. 'Well, I hope you'll be very happy,' she told him.

'And you, Julia?'

'Oh, I can't wait to do something I've wanted to do for so long...'

'And what is that?'

'Be independent.' How easy it was to tell fibs, she reflected, when one was desperate.

'Ah, yes, of course. I must wish you every success.' He bent his head and kissed her then. A kiss to drive all thoughts of independence out of her head. But he didn't wait for that. He pushed her gently through the door and closed it behind her, and she stood in the hall, listening to the gentle purring of the Rolls as he drove away.

She wasn't going to cry, she told herself, creeping silently to her room to hang up the pretty dress she supposed she would never wear again before getting into bed to weep silently all over Muffin, who had crept up with her. He was Ruth's cat now, but he had a strong affection for Julia and bore patiently with her snuffles and sighs.

Thomas had already left for the hospital by the time she got down to breakfast. Ruth took one look at her face and turned her back to make the toast.

'Did you have a lovely evening? We didn't hear you come in. Was the food good? I suppose it was all rather grand?'

'Well, it was, but you didn't notice it, if you see what I mean. It's a beautiful restaurant and the food was marvellous. It was a lovely evening.'

A remark which Ruth took with a pinch of salt, although she said nothing.

'Monica phoned yesterday evening. I'm to tell you that you're to go there if there is any kind of hitch at Sherborne. You have got everything fixed up?'

'Yes, I'll stay at a bed and breakfast place while I get the shop ready and buy some furniture. That ought not to take too long.'

She had been to a wholesaler and ordered her stock, packed her bags once more and there was nothing to keep her in London. And the Professor had gone back to Holland. The sooner she started her new life the better.

It was raining and chilly when she reached

Sherborne, and she was glad that the estate agent had been kind enough to recommend a place where she could stay. She had arranged to go there for a week, but probably it would be longer than that...

The house was in the centre of the town, one of a row of stone-built cottages of a fair size, and when the taxi stopped before its door Julia thought how cosy it looked. But the lady who answered the door didn't look cosy; she was immaculately dressed, not a hair out of place, a no longer youthful face carefully made up. Mrs Legge-Boulter welcomed Julia with chilly courtesy and within five minutes had made it clear that only most unfortunate circumstances had forced her to take in guests.

'It is not at all what I've been used to,' she observed, 'but beggars cannot be choosers, can they?' She laughed, but since she didn't look in the least amused Julia murmured in a non-committal manner as she was led upstairs to her room.

'I serve breakfast at half past eight,' said Mrs Legge-Boulter, 'and my guests are expected to be out of the house by ten o'clock. You may return after six o'clock. At the moment you are the only guest, so you may use the bathroom between nine and ten o'clock in the evening.'

'You don't offer evening meals?' said Julia hopefully.

Her landlady looked affronted. 'My dear Miss Gracey, you can have no idea of the work entailed in providing a room and breakfast for my guests. I am totally exhausted at the end of my day.'

Left alone, Julia examined her room. It was furnished with everything necessary for a bedroom, but the colour scheme was a beige and brown mixture unrelieved by ornaments or pictures. A place to sleep, decided Julia, and hoped that breakfast would be substantial. The sooner she could move into her little shop the better.

She unpacked her things and, since it was mid-afternoon, went into the town. She had tea and then went to take another look at her future home. Tomorrow she would see the estate agent and ask if he would let her have the key. She had signed the papers and paid over the money for the lease and the first month's rent. She sat over tea, making a list of all the things which had to be done, and then she wandered round the shops, looking for second-hand furniture and the mundane household equipment she would need. She earmarked several items, and then went in search of somewhere she could get her supper.

She found a small café near the abbey, serving light meals until eight o'clock, and she sat over a mushroom omelette and French fries and a pot of coffee until closing time and then returned to Mrs Legge-Boulter's house.

That lady opened the door to her with a thin smile, a request that she should wipe her feet and a reminder that breakfast was at half past eight. 'I must ask you to be punctual; I have my day to organise.'

Not only her day, reflected Julia, mounting the stairs, but the day of any unfortunate soul lodging with her. She had a bath and, mindful of the notice on the door, cleaned it and went to bed. She had a good deal to think about; the next few days were going to be fully occupied. But when she finally closed her eyes she allowed herself to think of Gerard. Even though she never intended to see him again, there was no reason why she shouldn't dream a little of what might have been...

She was tired, so that she slept well, and when she woke her only thoughts were concerned with getting down to breakfast. It was a frugal meal, served by Mrs Legge-Boulter with disdain, as though offering a boiled egg and two slices of toast was an affront to her social status. A miserable meal, decided Julia, gobbling everything in sight and shocking her landlady by asking for more hot water. The tea was already weak...

She left the house before ten o'clock, saw the estate agent, got the shop key and, fortified by coffee and a bun, let herself into what was now, for the moment, her property.

Not a great deal needed doing, she decided. A carpenter for the shop fittings, carpeting for the living room, and a good clean everywhere. So she went to the shops and returned presently with a bucket, broom, dusters and cleaning materials and set to. She paused for lunch and then went in search of a carpenter and a carpet shop.

It took a good deal of the afternoon but she found a carpenter who would come in the morning and also someone who would come and measure the floors. She went back to the café for a meal and then made her way back to Mrs Legge-Boulter's house, where she received the same tepid welcome as before. Really, thought Julia, lying in a hot bath and eating potato crisps, one wondered why her landlady chose to have lodgers when she obviously disliked them so much.

Breakfast was a boiled egg again. At least I shall get slim, thought Julia, and wondered if Gerard might like her better if she wasn't so curvy. A stupid thought, she told herself; he didn't like her whatever shape she was. She might be deeply in love, but it had made no difference to her appetite; she was still hungry when she left the house, and went along to the shop armed with a bag of currant buns, still warm from the oven at the bakers. Munching them, she went round the little place again, quite clear in her head as to what needed doing, so that by the time the carpenter arrived no time was lost. The floors measured, she took herself off to choose carpets, persuading everyone that everything had to be done as quickly as possible. A good morning's work, she decided, eating a splendid lunch in a friendly pub.

Buying a sewing machine and material for curtains took up her afternoon; tomorrow she would get them made and go in search of furniture. Hopefully she would be able to move in by the end of a week…

She had been busy all day, so that it had been fairly easy to forget Gerard. But now, back in her unwelcoming room, she forgot all about the shop and thought only of him. It wouldn't do, she told herself, sitting up in bed making yet another list. The sooner she got the shop open and had her hands full, the better. All the same, before she slept, in her mind's eye she roamed through the house in Amsterdam, remembering its age-old beauty and the endless quiet. She supposed that she would never forget them. She allowed herself a moment to wonder what Gerard was doing before she slept.

He was sitting in his magnificent drawing room and his mother was sitting opposite him, drinking after-dinner coffee by the small fire, for the evenings were cool.

Mevrouw van der Maes was a tall, imposing woman, elegantly dressed, not showing her age save for her white hair, worn in a French pleat. She had good looks still, and bright blue eyes. She sipped her coffee.

'This is delightful, Gerard; I see you so seldom. That can't be helped, I know. Den Haag is only half an hour's drive away, but that's too far if you've had a long day at the hospital. But I wish I saw more of you.'

'I'm thinking of cutting down on my work in England—not the London hospital but some of the provincial ones.'

'That means that you will make your home base here?' his mother asked, and added, 'You are thinking of getting married at last?'

He smiled. 'I've taken my time, haven't I? But, yes, that is my intention.'

'Do I know her? Oh, my dear, I shall be so happy…'

'An English girl; you may remember I mentioned her coming over here to look after Mrs Beckett?'

'And Nanny loved her, as I'm sure I shall. You will bring her to see me?'

'In a while, I hope.'

Something in his voice made her ask, 'She knows that you want to marry her?'

'No. When we first met it was hardly on the best of terms, and she has been at great pains to let me know that she is indifferent to me. At times she has allowed me to think that she likes me at least, but I think that has been due to circumstances...'

Mevrouw van der Maes asked quietly, 'You have told her that you love her?'

'No, and I've been careful not to show my feelings.'

His mother sighed silently. She loved Gerard deeply, and she was proud of him, his brilliant career, his good looks, his complete lack of pride in his success—and yet despite all those he was behaving like an uncertain youth in love for the first time. Men are so tiresome at times, reflected Mevrouw van der Maes.

There were a great many questions she wanted to ask him, but they must wait. When he had anything to tell her he would do so. Instead she began to talk about family matters.

The Professor, in Holland for a number of consultations, lectures and meetings with colleagues, found time to visit Mrs Beckett. He found her quite her old self again.

'Well, now,' said Nanny, offering a cheek for his kiss, 'how nice to see you, Mr Gerard. Miss Thrisp has been away for a week and I'm ripe for a gossip.'

So he told her all the news and gossip he knew that she enjoyed.

'And what's this I hear about Julia? She writes to me, bless her, but never a word about herself until this very day.' Mrs Beckett got out her specs. 'I had a letter this morning. Dear knows what the girl is doing—opening a shop, if you please. Full of plans, as bright as a button—and such nonsense. Why, she should be getting herself a husband instead of setting up on her own...'

The Professor asked casually, 'And where is this shop to be?'

'Sherborne—that's a small town in Dorset.' She took the letter from a pocket and re-read it. 'She's going to sell wools and embroidery and suchlike, and do a bit of dressmaking if there's a chance.'

Nanny turned the page. 'Here's a bit I missed. What does it say?'

She read it and looked worriedly at the Professor. 'She says not to tell anyone where she is—and now I've told you, Mr Gerard.'

He said placidly, 'Don't worry, Nanny, I won't tell a soul. I'm glad she still writes to you and that she appears to have such a bright future.'

'Future?' said Mrs Beckett pettishly. 'Nonsense. A lovely girl like her, selling wool to old ladies...' She added, 'And I thought you were taken with her...'

She looked at him, sitting at his ease, Jason at his feet, and saw his grin. And then she smiled herself while thoughts crowded into her elderly head: a wedding, babies and small children coming to stay with old Nanny.

But all she said was, 'Well, you've taken your time, Mr Gerard.'

CHAPTER NINE

SPURRED on by Julia, the carpenter made shelves and did some small repairs while two men laid a carpet in the living room; two more came to install a small gas stove and a gas fire. The little place was wired for a telephone and she had been promised that she would be connected as soon as possible. Everything was going smoothly, she thought with satisfaction, and took herself off to buy furniture.

She has already found a second-hand furniture shop down a small street, and she spent almost an hour there, searching out a nice small round table and two straight-backed chairs, a bookcase and a rather battered oak stand to hold a table lamp. She chose a chest of drawers too, and an old-fashioned mirror to go with it, and another little table which would do for a bedside stand with a lamp. Pleased with her purchases, she went back into the main street and bought a small easy chair. It cost rather more than she had expected, as did the padded stool for the bedroom and the bed, but she reminded herself that she could afford it.

She stopped for lunch presently, and then went in search of bed linen, towels and tablecloths, pots and pans, cutlery and all the small odds and ends which make up a home. She was tired by the evening, but she was getting everything done so far without a hitch; she slept like a proverbial log in her unwelcoming room and went downstairs in the morning to eat the inevitable egg, her head full of what still had to be done.

The little shop was ready to receive its contents; the first consignment of wool arrived that afternoon and she spent a long time arranging it on the shelves the carpenter had made. And some of the furniture had been delivered.

She saw Mrs Legge-Boulter, who, told that Julia would be leaving the next day, said with an unkind little titter, 'Well, I hope you won't regret opening a shop. I'm sure there isn't much call for wools and embroidery and so on, and that's not in the best shopping area.'

Julia, tired and to tell the truth a bit frightened of the future, said airily, 'I dare say I shall make more of a success of it than you with your bed and breakfast trade.'

To which Mrs Legge-Boulter took thin-lipped exception. 'Not a *trade*, Miss Gracey,' she explained coldly. 'A perfectly genteel way in which gentlefolk may add to their income.'

'Well, you're not adding much, are you?' observed Julia tartly. 'You'd do much better to put a few flowers in the rooms and offer some bacon for breakfast.'

She took herself off to bed and spent the next hour feeling ashamed of herself. She would apologise in the morning.

Which she did, for she was a kind-hearted girl even if her temper was a little out of hand at times. Her landlady ignored the apology, reminded her that she must be out of the house by ten o'clock and offered a boiled egg, not quite cold and rock-solid, and toast burnt at the edges.

There was no sign of her when Julia left the house. She had presented the bill at breakfast, waited while Julia paid, and then gone out of the room without a word.

A bad start to the day, thought Julia, although it had its funny side too. Only there was no one to laugh with her about it—the Professor for preference...

But once in the little room behind the shop she felt better. The odds and ends of furniture and the cheerful carpet and curtains made it quite cosy. She went into the tiny kitchen and arranged her few saucepans on the wall shelf and put the kettle on for a cup of coffee. There was no room for a table, only a worktop over the two small cupboards. Later, she promised herself, she would give the walls a coat of cheerful paint. She went through the shower room and loo and opened the back door. The patch of garden outside was neglected but the fences were sound and there was plenty of room for a wash-line.

The day went quickly; by the time she had made her bed and unpacked her things it was noon. She stocked her cupboard after lunch, made a cup of tea and sat by the gas fire drinking it. Tomorrow she would arrange the window, and then she would open the shop.

She phoned Ruth and Monica in the morning, after a sound night's sleep in her new bed, and warned them that until she had the phone connected they weren't to worry if she didn't ring for a day or two. The nearest phone box wasn't far away, but it would mean locking up the shop to go to it and she didn't want to miss the chance of a customer.

The window looked attractive, she thought: a small

display of knitting wools, embroidery silks and patterns, tapestry for canvas work, a little pyramid of coloured sewing thread... She sat behind the counter and watched people passing. Some stopped to look in but no one came into the shop. 'Well,' said Julia, 'I didn't expect anyone on the first day.'

Ruth and Monica had sent cards of good wishes, and Mrs Beckett had sent her a letter. The Professor, apprised of the opening date by Nanny, had restrained himself from rushing out and ordering six dozen red roses.

Julia had her first customer on the following day; an elderly woman came in and, after deliberation, bought a reel of sewing thread.

Her first customer and hopefully the start of many more.

Julia closed her little shop for the day and had tea and crumpets round the fire. The days were drawing in and the evenings were chilly; the housewives of Sherborne would be thinking of quiet evenings with their knitting or embroidery...

She hadn't expected instant success, but as the days went by with a mere trickle of customers her initial euphoria gave way to doubts which she did her best to keep at bay. Perhaps the ladies of Sherborne didn't knit? Perhaps they needed a little encouragement? She dressed the little window in a different fashion, with half-finished knitting arranged with careful carelessness in the corner, an almost complete tapestry opposite, and between them a basket filled with everything a knitter or needlewoman might need. And that brought customers—not many, not nearly enough!—but it was early days yet, she told herself.

Monica and George drove over to see her, and she led them round the shop and house, assuring them that everything was fine and that she was happier than she had been for years.

'So why does she look like that?' demanded Monica of her George as they drove back home. 'As though her world has come to an end? Oh, I know she was laughing and talking nineteen to the dozen, but that's not like her.' She frowned. 'Do you suppose...?'

George said, 'I agree that she isn't happy, but since she was at such pains to conceal that from us I feel that we should respect that.'

'She's in love,' said Monica, to which George said nothing. He was fond of his sister-in-law but she was a fiercely independent young woman. Any efforts to alter that, he considered, weren't for him or her sisters.

Monica, on the phone to Ruth, voiced her concern. 'And George says we mustn't interfere,' she added, with which Ruth agreed.

She wouldn't interfere, but she might drop a hint. She couldn't help but notice that whenever she saw the Professor he never once mentioned Julia. Ruth, sharing Mevrouw van der Maes' opinion that the best of men could be tiresome at times, bided her time.

A senior consultant at the hospital was retiring and she and Thomas had been invited to attend his farewell party—a sober affair, with sherry and morsels of this and that handed round on trays. Once the speeches had been made there was ample opportunity to mingle and chat. It took a little while to get the Professor to herself, and she wasted no time.

One or two remarks about the retiring consultant, a brief enquiry as to when Gerard would be going to Holland again, and then Ruth came to the point in what she hoped was a roundabout manner.

'So you're going to Holland...?'

She glanced up at him. He loomed over her, the picture of ease and she added, 'I expect you will go to your dear little cottage. That was a lovely holiday; Julia loved it too. She's quite settled, you know.'

'Sherborne is a charming little town, I'm told. I hear she has set up shop.'

Ruth gaped at him. 'You know? Who told you? She made us promise not to tell...'

He smiled down at her worried face. 'I thought that might be the case. It wasn't too difficult to discover where she was living.'

'Why do you want to know? I mean, you're not— that is, I didn't think that you liked each other much, even though you were always there when she needed someone.' She touched his sleeve. 'I'm sorry—I shouldn't have said anything. Only she's my sister and I love her very much.'

Two dignified members of the hospital committee were about to join them. 'So do I,' said the Professor gravely, and he turned to greet them.

She had no chance to speak to him again, and when a few days later she asked Thomas in a purposely vague manner if he had gone to Holland, Thomas answered just as vaguely that he was still at the hospital. 'Catching up on his work,' he added, but didn't mention that his chief was busy because he was planning a few days off.

Monica, at the other end of the phone, agreed that

there was nothing to be done. 'Julia can be as stubborn as a mule; if she got even a hint of all this she'd shut the shop and disappear. And as for Gerard, he'll sort everything out in his own good time. When you think about it, it's inevitable, isn't it? Only they've been at cross purposes ever since they met, haven't they? And they are so obviously suited to each other...'

A week later, on a fine, bright and chilly morning, the Professor bade Mrs Potts goodbye and, with Wilf and Robbie curled up in the back of the car, drove away from London going west.

Julia, totting up the week's takings, had to admit that business was slow. There had been several customers but none of them had bought more than a skein of wool or some embroidery silks. Even her simple arithmetic told her that she was running at a loss... And she had been open for three weeks now.

She rearranged the window display and added a notice that garments could be knitted, telling herself that it might be several months before she was established, then she made herself a cup of coffee, determined not to be downhearted.

She was rewarded not half an hour later by a customer who bought three ounces of wool and some knitting needles, and she was followed by a cross-looking woman who wanted a knitting pattern. She spent a long time sifting through the little pile Julia offered her, choosing with as much care as someone spending hundreds of pounds on a purchase. She still hadn't made up her mind when the shop door opened again and the Professor walked in.

Julia gave a gasp and the woman looked round and then back at the patterns. None of them, she told Julia, were what she wanted. She would do better if she went to a larger shop. And she swept out of the door.

The Professor eased his bulk from the door to the counter, his head bowed to prevent it coming in contact with the ceiling, and the little place was all at once overcrowded.

He said blandly, 'I hope that the rest of your customers are more profitable than that one!'

Julia glared at him. Her heart had turned over and leapt into her throat and she had only just managed to get it back where it belonged. She supposed that being in love made one feel giddy. But she was cross too; walking in like that without so much as a 'hello'—and if he hadn't then the woman might have bought something.

He leaned on the counter, disarranging the pile of patterns.

He said, 'You ran away...'

'I did no such thing. I have always wanted to own a shop and be independent...'

He leaned over the counter, opened the till drawer and looked at the handful of small change in it. 'Well,' he observed genially. 'You own a shop, but are you independent? Is that today's takings?'

It was a temptation to fib, but somehow she couldn't lie to him even if it was about something trivial. She said, 'The week's.'

He closed the drawer. 'It's a lovely day; will you have lunch with me?' And when she hesitated he asked, 'Have you ever been to Stourhead? There's a splendid lake there, with ducks and magnificent trees and all the peace in the world.'

He smiled slowly. 'Just for an hour or two? You must close for lunch; an extra hour won't make too much difference.'

'Well, it would be nice, but I must be back for the afternoon.'

She came from behind the counter and turned 'Open' to 'Closed' on the door, and asked, with her back to him, 'Are you on holiday?'

'Yes, for a day or two.'

'You aren't going to Holland?'

'Yes, but not immediately.'

She said, 'I won't be long—I must get a jacket.' She opened the door to the living room. 'If you'll wait here...'

She left him there and went up to her room, found a jacket and sensible shoes, poked at her hair and added lipstick and went downstairs. She was out of her mind, she told herself, seeing him sitting in the armchair, looking as though he belonged there. She wondered why he had come and how he had known where she was. Perhaps he intended to tell her that he was going back to Holland for good, to marry and live in his lovely old house in Amsterdam.

Doubtless she would be told over their lunch.

He had parked the car at the end of the little street and she was surprised and pleased to see Wilf and Robbie side by side in the back of the Rolls.

The Professor popped her into the car and got in beside her.

'We'll go to Stourhead; these two need a good walk.' He drove out of the town carrying on the kind of conversation which needed no deep thought and few replies. Their way took them through a quiet countryside with few villages and only the small town of Wincanton halfway. It was a bright day, and autumn had coloured the trees and hedges. The approach to the estate, with tantalising glimpses of its magnificent trees and shrubs over the high stone wall bordering the narrow road, was like a great tunnel, opening into a narrow lane leading to the gates.

There was a pub on one side, and a house or two on the other, and Gerard turned into the car park by the pub.

'We can lunch here. Shall we have coffee and then take the dogs for a walk? There's plenty of time.'

'Yes, please, I'd like that. Will Wilf and Robbie be allowed inside?' She looked down at the two whiskered faces and said, 'I never imagined that you would have dogs like these two.' And then went red because she had spoken her thoughts out loud and they had sounded rude.

He smiled a little. 'Neither did I; sometimes things happen whether one wants them or not. I wouldn't part with them now for a small fortune.'

They were walking to the pub entrance. 'And they're company for Mrs Potts when you're in Holland. Will you take them with you when you leave England?'

'They will go where I go,' he told her, and opened the pub door.

There was no one in the bar, but the cheerful man who was stacking glasses wished them good day and had no objection to Wilf and Robbie—and certainly, he told them cheerfully, they could have coffee.

I shouldn't be here, reflected Julia. I ought not to have come. But she knew that nothing would have stopped her; she felt as though she had left her mundane life behind and had gone through a door into a world where there was no one but Gerard. And this really is the last time, she told herself, forgetting how many times she had already said that.

The Professor, watching her thoughts showing so clearly on her face, had his own thoughts, but all he said was, 'Shall we go? If we walk all round the lake it will take an hour or so.'

There was a church by the pub, small and old, and while Gerard got their tickets from the kiosk at the gate she wandered up the path between the ancient tombstones and peered through its open door. It was beautiful inside, quiet with the quietness of centuries, and there were flowers everywhere. Presently she felt the weight of Gerard's arm on her shoulders and they stood together without speaking, then turned and went down the path together.

The dogs were waiting patiently, so they each took a lead and started along the path round the lake, not hurrying; there was too much to see—towering trees, bushes and shrubs, ducks on the water and, hidden away from the path, Grecian temples and presently a waterfall, and a wooden bridge under which there were shoals of small fish. They didn't talk much, but every now and then Julia clutched Gerard's arm to point out something she wanted him to see.

There weren't many people there and it was quiet save for the birds. They found the grotto presently, at the bottom of narrow steps, and then walked the short distance back to the gates.

There were a few people in the pub now, but they found a table in a window and Wilf and Robbie, refreshed with water and a biscuit, curled up at their feet while they ate a Ploughman's lunch and emptied a pot of coffee. And Julia, munching warm bread and cheese, didn't think of the past or the future, only the happy present.

She looked up and caught his eye. 'I feel happy,' she told him seriously, a remark which brought a gleam to his eye.

He drove her back to Sherborne presently, talking easily about their walk, and discussing what they had seen. When they got to the shop, he got out and unlocked the door for her, listened to her thanks, assured her that he had enjoyed himself as much as she had and then bade her a cheerful goodbye.

She watched him drive away and went through the shop and sat down in the living room. She wanted very much to have a good cry, but a customer might come. No one came. She locked the door at half past five and made herself a pot of tea. She wasn't hungry, and the memory of the Ploughman's lunch, eaten so contentedly in the Professor's company, would serve for her supper.

Of course she didn't sleep; she lay awake thinking of him driving back to London. He had had a free day and, having discovered where she was, had made her the purpose of a drive into the country. He had wished her goodbye in a most casual manner; now he had seen for himself where she was he would lose all interest—if he'd had any in the first place. But he had been kind to her on several occasions; perhaps he felt under an obligation to Thomas...

She dropped off to sleep at last and woke with a start. The shop doorbell was ringing—the postman must be getting impatient. She got into her dressing gown and slippers and hurried to the door, not stopping to pull up the blind.

Wilf and Robbie trotted in, and hard on their heels was the Professor. He shut the door behind him, turned the key in the lock and then stood for a moment, looking down at her sleepy face and tangled mane of hair. He had had a sleepless night too, but there was no sign of that in his quiet face.

He gathered her into his arms. 'Tell me truly,' he begged. 'Are you happy here?'

She shook her head against his chest.

'Then would you consider marrying me? I have waited patiently for you to make a career for yourself, for it seemed to me that that was what you wanted more than anything else. But there is a limit to a man's patience and I am at the end of mine. But you have only to say, Go away, and I will go.'

Julia sniffed back tears as she mumbled, 'Don't go. Please don't go.' And then, 'You shouldn't be here; its seven o'clock in the morning. And if you love me, why didn't you say so? And I don't want to be independent. Only there wasn't anything else and I thought you didn't like me.'

'My darling,' said the Professor soothingly. 'Let us get one thing straight. I fell in love with you when we first met, although perhaps I didn't realise that at once. I have never stopped loving you and I never shall.'

'Really?' She looked up into his face and smiled at what she saw there.

'Really,' said the Professor, and bent to kiss her.

It was quite a while before she went upstairs to dress, leaving Gerard to put the kettle on and let the dogs into the little back garden. Her head was a jumble of thoughts: they would marry just as soon as possible; she would go back to London with him that morning; she was not to worry about the shop, he would deal with that; they would live in his lovely old house in Amsterdam. But none of these were important. The one thought which filled her head was that he loved her. She bundled up her hair, dashed powder on her nose and ran downstairs to tell him once again that she loved him too.

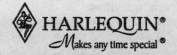

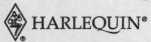
HARLEQUIN®

makes any time special—online...

eHARLEQUIN.com

your romantic escapes

—Indulgences—

♥ Monthly guides to indulging yourself, such as:
- ★ Tub Time: A guide for bathing beauties
- ★ Magic Massages: A treat for tired feet

—Horoscopes—

♥ Find your daily Passionscope, weekly Lovescopes and Erotiscopes

♥ Try our compatibility game

—Reel Love—

♥ Read all the latest romantic movie reviews

—Royal Romance—

♥ Get the latest scoop on your favorite royal romances

—Romantic Travel—

♥ For the most romantic destinations, hotels and travel activities

If you enjoyed what you just read,
then we've got an offer you can't resist!

Take 2 bestselling love stories FREE!

Plus get a FREE surprise gift!

Harlequin Romance®

EXTRA!!! 𝕿𝖍𝖊 𝕿𝖎𝖒𝖊𝖘 **EXTRA!!!**

Runaway Bride Seeks Affair To Remember!

Do you like stories that get
up close and personal?

Do you long to be loved *truly, madly, deeply?*

Ever wondered what Harry *really* thought of Sally?

**If you're looking for emotionally
intense, tantalizingly tender love stories,
stop searching and start reading:**

**LIZ FIELDING
JESSICA HART
RENEE ROSZEL
SOPHIE WESTON**

They're fresh, flirty and feel-good.

Look out for their latest novels,
coming soon to Harlequin Romance®.

HARLEQUIN®
Makes any time special ®

Visit us at www.eHarlequin.com

HRRS

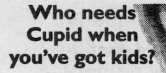

Strong and silent...
Powerful and passionate...
Tough and tender...

Who can resist the rugged loners of the Outback?
As tough and untamed as the land they rule, they
burn as hot as the Australian sun once they meet
the woman they've been waiting for!

Feel the Outback heat throughout 2002 when
these fabulous authors

Margaret Way
Barbara Hannay
Jessica Hart

bring you:

Men who turn your whole world upside down!